Tiare
x

WOMEN OF THE WILD

Copyright © 2017 MADA books
All rights reserved. This book or any portion thereof
may not be reproduced or used in any manner
whatsoever without the express written permission of
the publisher except for the use of brief quotations in a
book review or scholarly journal.
First edition printed: 2017
ISBN 978 1 9742 8743 7
www.madabooks.com

Contents

Storm Warning by Diane Enderby	pg. 1
Good Teeth by Evangeline Chateau-Loney	pg. 2
The Smile Maidens by S. E. Cyborski	pg. 6
Radio Grandma by Helen Noble	pg. 26
The Durga by L. S. Reinholt	pg. 47
Warren Womb by Alex Clarke	pg. 57
Queen of the Animals by Gemma Cartmell	pg. 62
Freedom to Lie by Casey Armstrong	pg. 76
The Fox Mother by Emmy Clarke	pg. 93
Refuge by Ruth Woodward	pg. 95
Meet the Storytellers	pg. 101

STORM WARNING
BY DIANE ENDERBY

Sit with me in the eye of the storm
We can rest until morning together
I feel the weather in your beating heart
Connecting your body to mine with a torrent of love
A current too strong for a child to endure
So let's watch
The water pour and
Listen to the rain on our faces
And while the roofs fly off houses and
Tall buildings crash to the ground
You can sleep in the serenity
Of my arms

GOOD TEETH
BY EVANGELINE CHATEAU-LONEY

When I was little, my mum used to say that I had "good teeth". Every six months without fail, I'd come out of the dentist's with a garish sticker that read "WELL DONE" peeling from my school jumper, and a sparkly-clean bill of health. The receptionist would always pat me on the head and greet me as "wee lamb" when my mum came up to the desk to sign the forms. I hated being called "wee lamb", and I hated being patted on the head. My hair was of the sort that stuck out thickly in all directions, and the receptionist's rings always got caught in it.

The dentist's surgery was in a little converted cottage near the centre of our smart, green, well-to-do village, and my mum would park the car by the church and go do the shopping while I was in having my check-up. On the way home afterwards she would always produce some sort of odd after-school snack for me; sesame snaps, or a round flat muffin shedding its white floury coating into a paper bag, or a clootie dumpling from the butcher. I enjoyed the dumplings best, because they were like the fruitcake we got at Christmas but gooier, and you could tear them apart and chew on them for ages and make a right mess.

It was usually while I was munching away in the back of the car that my mum would start up about my having "good teeth", and how I'd inherited them from my Granny, who'd never had a filling in all her born days. After the mention of my teeth, this talk would go one of two ways. Either my mum would comment that Granny also had "good hair" (in other words, she never went grey) and go on about Granny's home in the forests of Argyll and how it was a wonderful place for a growing bairn like me, or she would bring up The Photo again.

The Photo, as I thought of it with weary resignation, was of myself at age three-and-three-quarters, with my floppy sunhat that I refused to take off and my squinty eye that hadn't been operated on yet, sitting pleased as Punch in my high-chair in our old house, gnawing on an enormous ham bone. Although I'd seen it many a time in one of our ancient family albums, my mum loved to bring it up as if I hadn't. My dad, who'd taken the wretched thing in the first place, never seemed to tire of telling my aunts and uncles about it when they came to visit. The Photo was always greeted with earnest nods from them, and oh yes I definitely had good teeth just like my Granny and wasn't I lucky.

Well, I'm not sure how much of it was luck, really. It wasn't that I ate fewer sweets or brushed more; it was just that my Granny's genes seemed to be strong enough that I escaped the agony of fillings and the humiliation of braces, both of which were par for the course among my friends. I can clearly recall the glum, numb expression of my best friend Tilly, arriving an hour after school had started one pouring wet Tuesday, her faced encased in a lurid pink plastic contraption. I was horrified to learn that day that she would have to wear the monstrosity for three whole months, and couldn't even take it off to go to sleep at night.

The summer I was eleven, my parents decided to do the house up, and that I ought to be on holiday at Granny's while that was going on. They seemed to feel that I wasn't getting enough fresh air and exercise, and it was true that the adults who had previously called me "wee lamb" now commented worriedly on how whey-faced and sickly I looked. My sleep schedule was all over the place even for an excitable growing girl, and I'm pretty sure it was around that time that I started having all sorts of problems with my hair. No matter what anyone did to it, it grew out long and tangly and tough as wire, and several pairs of hairdresser's scissors snipped their last trying to tame it. Dad even wanted to take me to some sort of specialist at one point, but my mum put her foot down, saying that there was no reason for fuss and that being at Granny's would do me the world of good. I can't blame her really, as Granny was her mother after all, and even my dad always said I took after mum's side of the family more.

At first I didn't want to leave home and my friends for a whole summer, but in the end it worked out fine. My sleep went back to normal, and so did my hair. I've been visiting Granny every month for about a year now, and it's been great. She knows a whole lot of really interesting stuff about the natural world, so I'm being educated even when I'm not in school, and staying in the forest has really made me appreciate it up close.

Granny and I have a lot of the same hobbies, and though the cottage is remote, we do sometimes get friendly hikers or map-wielding tourists passing by. Usually, they're ramblers following the nature trail, laden with poorly-rolled sleeping bags and way too many walking poles. Granny always invites them in for tea and biscuits, and they often have interesting stories to tell about the lives they've lived. Some of them are kind of doddery, but that's not necessarily a bad thing, as they're inevitably slower to react. Being elderly also means they can get a bit stringy, but Granny and I don't mind a bit of gristle. After all, we have good teeth.

The Smile Maidens
by S. E. Cyborski

Have you ever heard of the smile maidens? I'd never heard of them before my travels and, at the beginning, I'd scoffed at the idea of them. It seemed such a silly name for a supernatural force that killed people or stole their souls. I'd made a study of the supernatural before I'd started traveling and nowhere mentioned anything like them. But I'm getting ahead of myself.

It started in a blustery village sometime late in October. The moon was wending her way towards full, her white form growing each night. The night I heard of the smile maidens, the moon was as close to full as to make no difference and the white light gleamed over the bare branches of twisted trees. I huddled into my scarf and hiked my bag further up on my back. A warm glow in the distance told me I had nearly reached my destination: a tavern that served as a bed and breakfast in the area. I hurried my steps, craving the warmth that glow in the distance offered. There were two cars parked outside the building, both looking unremarkable and dark in the moonlight.

When I stepped inside the tavern, the scent of oak burning in a fire and a savory roast filled my nose. I breathed deeply and let out a happy sigh. Lunch had been a long time ago and I was starving. The warmth of the room infused my body and I started unwrapping myself from my scarf and coat. There were few patrons in the tavern tonight. A surly-looking elderly man sat on a stool at the bar, nursing a half-empty glass. The fire sparkled through the amber liquid inside the glass. The bartender and, I assumed, manager was standing off to the side of the man, wiping down the counter with a rag. Across the way, a chessboard between them, two women sat at a table. Both women had a glass by their elbow, mostly empty now. One was filled with what looked like water and the other was filled with the same amber liquid as the surly-looking man's.

"Help ya?" the bartender asked shortly, glancing my way with a bit of curiosity in his eyes.

"Yeah, I was told there were rooms for the night here?"

"We got rooms," the man nodded and a curt smile pulled at his lips for a moment. "Slow night so take your pick."

"Um, how about one with a window?" I asked. I didn't like spending time in rooms without windows. They always made me feel trapped, like I couldn't breathe. "How much for the night?"

"Forty bucks for the night," the man said, plucking a key from a hook on the wall behind him. I saw four other hooks with keys on them. "All the rooms got windows."

He plunked the key down on the bar and held out a hand. I dug out my cash, counting out rumpled tens and handing over forty dollars. It seemed a bit pricey, especially considering other places like this I'd stayed at. Then again, this was the only place to get a room within a comfortable walking distance and it was getting late. My stomach grumbled again as a door off to the side of the bar opened and a woman sailed out with two plates piled high with roast and vegetables.

"Dinner's part of the fee," the man said as the woman set the plates down in front of the other two women. They paused in their game to thank her. "Just let Susie know if you'd like a plate and she'll bring it out."

"Thanks." I nodded, picked up the key and headed towards the stairs. I watched Susie sail back into the kitchen and her cheerful whistling was cut off by the door closing. I looked at my key and saw a room number on it.

Heading upstairs, I saw that the rooms were lined up off the hallway. The hallway went all the way to the back of the building. There was a window about halfway down and I paused at it, looking outside and taking deep breaths. Clouds drifted over the moon, obscuring the silver light and casting the world below into deep shadows. A movement caught my eye; something Cupid's bow-shaped that seemed to be moving against the wind. But when I focused on it, the moon came back out from behind the clouds. Nothing was there. I shook my head and laughed at myself. Seeing things in the darkness of a strange place! Nothing new and nothing to fear.

I opened the door to the last bedroom in the hallway, dumping my bag on the bed. The room was clean if sparsely furnished. The bed took up most of the space, leaving a small aisle around it to walk in. There was a window on the wall to the left of the bed and a wooden nightstand sat underneath it. There was a kerosene lamp on the nightstand along with matches. I didn't see any electric lights and smiled at that. There was a small dresser across from the bed and a rickety old chair sat next to the dresser. It didn't look like it would support me but I threw my coat and scarf on it. It rocked a little with the sudden weight but didn't break.

I sat down on the bed with a groan, the mattress

sinking underneath me with a wooden creaking sound. The frame was old, though not rickety like the chair. The quilt was soft; the scent of lavender and mint wafting up around me as I moved. It looked blue and gray in the moonlight filtering in through the window. I thought about lying down, my feet aching from the long hike today. But my stomach grumbled again, a little louder this time. Dinner it was, then.

I headed back downstairs, sitting a table away from the women playing chess. I studied them while I waited for Susie to reappear from the kitchen again. The older woman, comfortably plump and sitting straight-backed in her chair, had black hair liberally streaked with silver. It was pulled back by a gold clip at the base of her neck. Her sweater was black and looked fluffy and warm. Her jeans were tucked into gray boots that ended halfway up her legs. Her amber eyes were full of mischief as she moved one of her pawns to take her opponent's knight.

"Gotcha," the woman crowed in a contralto voice, the sound vibrant. "Let's see you get out of that one, Maria."

"I'm sure I'll figure something out, Ma," the younger woman, Maria, replied with a smile. "I can beat you about half the time, remember."

The older woman chuckled and I turned my attention to Maria. She had the same black hair as her mother, without the silver. Her eyes were a darker brown though they sparkled with delight just like her mother's. She wore a dark green sweater and jeans over hiking boots. Her hair wasn't pulled back but it was cut short. Gold studs glittered in her ears. She was more slender than her mother. As if sensing my attention, she turned to look at me. I gave her a small smile and a nod then jumped as Susie bustled up to my table. I hadn't even heard the door to the kitchen open.

"What can I get ya, dear?" Susie asked, giving me a maternal smile. "Got roast on but I can do sandwiches also. My husband, Amos there, can get ya what ya want to drink too."

"The roast sounds delicious," I said, unable to help smiling back. "And if I can get water from Amos, that'd be perfect."

As Susie walked away, Amos plunked down a filled glass on the table. He left without saying a word, going back to the bar and refilling the surly-looking man's glass. I took a drink, looking around the room for a few moments before my attention was pulled back to the chess game. Maria had moved her other knight nearly all the way over to the other side and was tapping a finger against the side of the board as her mother deliberated.

"Here we go," the older woman said, moving one of her bishops up two spaces. Then she looked over at me. "Know chess, hun?"

"A little," I replied, scooting my chair closer. "I know enough to play but that's about it. My dad taught me when I was little."

"Ma taught all of us when we were kids," Maria laughed, finger still tapping the board. "I have two older brothers and I was able to wipe the board with them before I was sixteen. Ma, however, I wasn't able to beat until I was in my twenties."

"Long experience and lots of play," the older woman laughed. She held out a hand for me to shake. "I'm Anna. Looks like you traveled a long way to get here tonight. You have a destination in mind?"

"No, not really," I replied, shaking Anna's hand. "I've been wandering mostly, collecting stories here and there. Eventually I want to head to the sea, sail somewhere else."

"Stories, huh? I know a few that would send you into frights," Anna said, leaning back in her chair and crossing her arms over her chest.

"Oh Ma, she doesn't want to hear about those old stories," Maria said, finally moving her rook forward. "They're just silly."

"What stories?" I asked at the same time Anna replied, "Course she does, Maria love. She just said she's collecting stories."

Susie interrupted us then, appearing with a plate of roast and vegetables for me. It smelled heavenly and my stomach rumbled in appreciation. She set the plate down with a wink and hurried off. I didn't waste any time before digging in, cutting off a piece of roast and shoving it in my mouth. I closed my eyes in sheer bliss. When I opened them again, I saw that Anna and Maria had set aside their game, the board carefully placed on the table next to them, and were working on their own dinners.

We ate in a companionable silence for a few minutes. I was hungrier than I'd expected and had to work not to just wolf down my food. It was the best meal I'd had in a week, even counting the other places I'd stopped for food. And it was far better than the rudimentary meals I'd made over the little campfires I'd cobbled together when I'd camped outside.

"So, old stories, yes?" Anna said some time later, pushing a small piece of potato around her plate with a fork. "Have you heard of the smile maidens yet?"

"'Smile maidens'?" I asked as I tilted my head to

the side. I didn't even need to check the notebook I'd left upstairs; the name wasn't familiar. "What are they?"

"A fairytale to scare kids into staying in bed at night," Maria snorted, voice full of derision. "It's the kind of story you tell alongside those of goblins and dragons and trolls."

"Which exist somewhere, don't they?" Anna asked sharply, though both women had the air of an argument old and comfortable and no longer heated. "Otherwise why would we have the stories? They warn us of the monsters."

"So they're a monster?" I asked, cutting into the argument. "What kind of monster?"

"No one knows for sure. No one's seen one," Anna said. She paused to pick up the piece of potato and eat it slowly. She stared into the fire, her eyes reflecting back golden flames. "At least, no one's survived to tell the tale. Except for one woman."

"Great-great-great-great-grandmother, right?" Maria said dryly, rolling her eyes. She fell silent as Anna sent her a glare, and ate a piece of roast.

"My great-great-great-grandmother was a passionate and headstrong young woman," Anna said, her voice falling into the cadence of a well-known tale told often. "Victoria her name was. And she was always butting heads with her parents. Victoria loved a boy in the village they lived in, a boy named William. He was the blacksmith's apprentice. William was a very quiet and shy boy, never putting himself in the light. Victoria claimed it was love at first sight."

"What happened?" I asked, enthralled by the story.

"Well, her parents didn't want her to marry

William, which Victoria had every intention of doing. They wanted her to marry the local judge's son. They'd spoken with the boy's father when Victoria and the boy were little, agreeing the children would be married when they came of age," Anna continued. She took a drink of her beer and stared into the flames for a few moments. Sadness came into her eyes then. "But Nathaniel, the judge's son, grew up ruthless and cruel. All the animals in the area were terrified of him. Anytime he walked the village, dogs ran in fear and the small animals completely disappeared. A few times, headless chickens or gutted dogs were found in dark alleys. No one came forward about the deaths but Victoria had noted a cruel glint in Nathaniel's eyes when he saw the bodies."

"Sounds like a bad person," I agreed. I ate some more of my dinner, washing it down with sips of water. I couldn't decide what made it so delicious. Maybe the spices? Or perhaps how it was cooked? "What did Victoria do?"

"She and William made plans to elope," Anna replied with a smile. "But two of Victoria's little sisters overheard their conversation. They went straight to their parents and told them. Then, their parents approached William. They were pretty well off and they offered him money if he'd leave without Victoria. It was more than he'd ever seen in his life and William accepted."

"That's terrible," I said, shaking my head.

"Yeah but it probably worked out for the best," Maria cut in. Her plate was almost empty now, as was her glass of water. "William died not too long after he left. A weak heart, according to the doctor."

"How do you know?" I asked, confused.

"Victoria looked into everything years later. She wanted to know what had happened to her first love," Anna explained. "It took her some time to piece it together and she never forgave her parents."

"That's a sad story. But I don't understand how it relates to these smile maidens," I said.

"I was just getting to that," Anna laughed. "Well, the day they were supposed to elope, Victoria went to the blacksmith. But William was gone, and no one knew where. She was heartbroken. That night, she went for a walk and ended up at a little pond outside the village. It was a cool night but not cold. The moon was just past full and clouds scudded across the sky. I don't think even Victoria knew what she was going to do. Throw herself into the water? Cry on the banks? Scream to an uncaring moon?"

"Maybe all or none?" I suggested and Maria laughed. "Maybe she just wanted some time alone?"

"Possibly. I suppose we'll never know," Anna said. She paused again to eat some more of her dinner. The silence stretched and I turned back to my own food. My stomach wasn't making its complaints known anymore but I was still hungry. I ate steadily until most of my dinner was gone. While we ate, Maria studied the board and moved another piece. Anna flicked a glance at the board and nodded at her daughter.

"I heard that masters of the game could tell who would win just by watching the first few moves," I said, pointing at the board with my chin. "Is that possible?"

"If you're really good and you know the strengths, weaknesses, and playing styles of the players, sure," Maria said while Anna continued to eat. "As for this game, I don't really know who's going to win. Like I said, I can beat Ma about half the time. We're pretty evenly matched though we have different styles."

"What do you mean?" I asked.

"I'm more aggressive a player than Ma is," Maria explained. "She's more content to sit back and let things develop. I like to make things develop."

"Which is part of why you lose to me so often," Anna laughed. She'd finished her plate now and was enjoying the last of her beer. "I can set traps for you that won't work on others."

Maria shook her head and smiled. She glanced at the board, a satisfied look in her eyes. I didn't really know what strategies might be in employ on the board but it looked like Maria believed she had a few traps of her own. I finished off the rest of my dinner and Susie came out of the kitchen again. She gave all of us a genial smile as she picked up our empty plates.

"There's peach pie for dessert, if anyone's in the mood for something sweet," she explained. "It's my own recipe and we've some fresh vanilla ice cream to go along with it."

Anna and I both asked for a slice while Maria declined. I got up in the lull in conversation and asked Amos to refill my glass of water. Maria followed suit, resting her arms on the bar as she stood next to me. Her perfume filled my nose, something flowery and bright. I glanced at her, noting how the fire illuminated the planes of her face. She was beautiful in that light. Amos put my glass on the bar in front of me with a thunk and I whipped my eyes to it. I picked it up with a word of thanks and headed back to my seat. Anna stared at me with a thoughtful look in her eyes that disappeared when Maria came back.

"So, where was I? Oh yes, Victoria on the bank of that pond," Anna said when Maria had settled herself and repositioned the board on their table. "She was heartbroken and angry and feeling betrayed. She had no idea yet that her parents had paid William off. She'd thought he'd just up and left her. A cloud floated over the moon, hiding the light and casting the pond into shadow. That's when Victoria saw it: a Cupid's bow-shaped shadow that flitted over the land to her left, following a natural hill. She thought nothing of it, maybe a leaf or a small night animal, until she realized that it was moving against the wind."

I shifted uncomfortably in my seat, suddenly reminded of the shadow I thought I'd seen earlier. It had been Cupid's bow-shaped and seemed to move against the wind. But it had disappeared before I'd gotten a good look at it. Surely it was just a shadow or a trick of the light? I took a deep drink of my water, trying to calm the nerves that suddenly erupted in my belly.

"The shadow moved closer and closer, though Victoria felt no fear at first," Anna continued, studying me closely. Had she noticed my squirming? "Then the cloud drifted away from the moon and light fell on the area. A woman stood in front of her, clothed in nothing but her long dark hair."

"Bet that was a shock," I murmured. "Where did the woman come from?"

"She was a smile maiden, though Victoria didn't know that yet," Anna said. "She asked Victoria what was wrong and Victoria explained the whole thing. The woman was silent for a time. Then she lifted her hand and held it out to Victoria. Her lips stretched into a parody of a smile and she asked if Victoria would come with her and help her. She could take the pain away in return. Victoria was about to take her hand when a cloud half covered the moon. The woman's hand disappeared as did most of her body. It turned to shadow while only her head and shoulders remained, still illuminated by the moon. Victoria screamed and ran. Another cloud fully covered the moon when Victoria looked back and saw that the Cupid's bow shadow was back. It chased her all the way home. Victoria slammed the door and huddled by the light of the fire. She didn't move until the sun rose the next morning."

"Weird. But the woman could have been playing a prank or something," I offered, shrugging. Susie had returned with our desserts about halfway through the last part of the story and I took a bite of pie and ice cream. "There's nothing to suggest she was one of these smile maidens."

"When Victoria told her mother what had happened, her mother turned white with fear and hugged Victoria close," Maria said, continuing the story. She just shook her head when Anna looked at her. "What? I know the story as well as you do. Eat your pie. I'll tell the rest."

"So her mother knew what Victoria was talking about?" I asked.

"The smile maidens are a story whispered about only on the brightest days. Some people were afraid that even mentioning them brought their attention to you," Maria explained. She sat back in her chair and rested her arms on her legs. "No one told the story to their children until they were adults themselves. It was why Victoria didn't know the story. She was still a little young to have heard it. Victoria's mother told her about the smile maidens then and how they could be avoided. They never came out in the light, whether the sun or firelight. They kept to the shadows, being made of shadow themselves. They always took the same shape, which is where their name came from. Their shadow was shaped like a smile. They could move along flat surfaces, anywhere a shadow might fall. And if moonlight fell on them, they turned into beautiful women. What they were, no one knew. Demon, ghost, fae? None of the above? But they were dangerous. Men, they killed. But women, women were another story. Should moonlight fall on a smile maiden while she was approaching a woman, she would try to take the woman and make *her* a smile maiden. It's said that any woman taken as a smile maiden would lose her soul in the process, it being eaten by the one turning her."

"That's disturbing." I shuddered, thinking again of the shadow I'd seen. While I didn't quite believe in the smile maidens, that wouldn't stop me from lighting the little kerosene lamp on my nightstand tonight. I finished my pie in a thoughtful silence. The fire crackled, keeping the room from being uncomfortably silent. The surly-looking man left and Amos wiped down the bar before heading into the kitchen. "Let's hope it doesn't give me nightmares."

"It did the first time I heard the story," Maria said, giving me a sympathetic smile. "But no one's seen or heard of one again. I personally think it's just a tale to frighten kids with."

Anna snorted. She and Maria played through the rest of their game while Susie bustled through the room cleaning up. She took our empty plates and glasses back to the kitchen where I heard sounds of water and splashing. Then she wiped down all the tables. After checking on the fire, she went back into the kitchen. I heard singing join the splashing, a homey and comfortable sound. A few minutes later, Anna let out a small sound of triumph.

"I thought I had you that time, Ma, I really did," Maria groaned, tipping over her king. "I didn't see that you'd sacrificed that bishop until it was too late."

"That's all right, Maria love, it's not a common move," Anna replied. She and Maria put the chess pieces away and left the box on the table. "And now," she said to me, "I think it's time we bid you goodnight. I hope you don't have nightmares but I wouldn't be surprised."

"Good night. It was a pleasure to have met you both," I said, shaking Anna's hand and then Maria's. Both women had strong grips though Maria's skin was softer than her mother's. They shrugged into their coats and started to leave. The shadow I'd seen earlier rose up in my memory and suddenly I wanted to warn them. I started forward, one hand raised. "Wait!"

"What is it?" Maria asked, a touch annoyed. She was standing in the open doorway, a cold breeze swirling about her legs.

"Um, just, you know, be careful," I said lamely, looking away from the two women. I shuffled my feet, embarrassed that I was trying to warn them about a fairytale. But still, I was pretty sure I had seen that shadow. And Anna was looking at me with a curious expression. "It's pretty dark out there. Be careful of – I don't know. Bats or something."

"Bats," Maria repeated flatly then shook her head. She walked outside, heading to the car parked out there.

Anna didn't follow her right away. "Be careful," she repeated my words slowly, as if tasting them. "Yes, we will. And I believe you should be careful yourself, tonight. Keep a light on."

I nodded, feeling a little less embarrassed. Anna studied me then nodded sharply. She called a goodnight that Susie answered cheerfully from the kitchen then headed out. The door closed, cutting off the cold breeze. A log cracked in the fireplace, startling a yelp out of me. I glared at the fire for a moment then shrugged. A yawn pulled at my jaw and I made up my mind to head to bed. I'd walked a lot today.

I retraced my steps to my room, taking a few minutes to get the kerosene lamp lit. Once it was, I lowered the wick until the flame threw a small pool of light around my bed. A short exploration of the hallway showed a bathroom just beyond my room. Then I got ready for bed. The wind blew around the building, whistling and calling as if trying to lure me out. I tuned it out as I headed back to my room. Undressing, I shivered in the slight chill and slid gratefully under the quilt. The scent of lavender and mint rose around me as the covers warmed to my body heat. I burrowed in happily, yawning again. I glanced at the kerosene lamp one more time, making sure it was still lit and wasn't likely to go tumbling. Then I was asleep.

I don't know how much time passed but, all of a sudden, I was wide awake. The kerosene lamp was still burning on the night stand. A golden pool of light surrounded my bed like a barrier. I looked up at the window and saw darkness. It was still night and, as there was no moonlight, more clouds must have rolled in. I turned over onto my back, rubbing at my eyes. That was what made me think that what I saw next was a trick of my eyesight at first.

In the corner of the room, a shadow moved slowly across the floor from the doorway. It crept towards my bed, a Cupid's bow-shape that didn't distort or change in the flickering light of the lamp. I caught my breath, wondering if I was seeing what I thought I was. Anna's story of the smile maidens ran through my head and I looked at the lamp again. I was safe in the light. I would be okay, even if that shadow that couldn't really be there was actually there. I pulled the covers up over my shoulders and determinedly shut my eyes.

Then I felt the gust of wind.

My eyes snapped open to darkness. The kerosene lamp had been blown out. The gust must have gotten in through a chink in the windowpane. But whatever happened, my room was now in darkness. I sat up in bed, shaking hands reaching for the matches I'd left next to the lamp. That was when I saw the shadow again. The Cupid's bow-shape seemed to stretch wider as it saw me. It was beside the nightstand. I watched; my eyes widening as the shadow flowed around the front and down to the floor. I leaned over the edge of the bed, trying to track it.

The next time I saw it, it was easing its way up the frame of the bed. I whimpered and drew my legs up to my chest. I wanted to run, to scream, anything to stop the implacable advance of that shadow. As I opened my mouth, the clouds rolled away from the moon.

It was even colder now; the sun's meager warmth a long-lost memory. The moon cast frozen beams of light into the room to limn everything in icy silver.

The shadow was gone. I breathed a sigh of relief, looking up at the window. I could see the moon, a glowing, round light in the heavens. I stretched my legs out again and dropped my eyes to the nightstand to look for the matches. It was then, out of the corner of my eye, that I saw the figure standing next to my bed. I froze, wanting to close my eyes and terrified to at the same time. Finally, I made myself look.

A woman stood next to my bed. She was tall, her eyes dark pools that seemed to draw in the silver light shining down on her. Her hair was dark, curling fetchingly around her shoulders and tickling the tops of her bare breasts. My eyes swept down her form and back up, realising she was naked. She was pale, skin seeming to glow nearly the same colour as the moonlight. Her skin looked smooth and soft, her limbs lushly round. She was breathtaking, ethereal and fey.

"All the other rooms are full," she murmured, her voice seeming to throb in the air. "And it's so very cold. May I share with you?"

She held a hand out to me entreatingly. It was cold in the room, a slight mist issuing from both our mouths as we breathed. Her skin was pebbled with goosebumps and she shivered where she stood. A small voice reminded me that Amos had said they had no other guests, but was quickly overrun by warm molasses coating my thoughts. Nothing else mattered but her voice. I managed a nod, lifting up the blanket. Cold air raised bumps on my own naked skin and I shivered.

She slipped into the bed gracefully, taking the blanket from my hand and draping it back over both of our bodies. I lay back down, crossing my arms over my chest and keeping very still. The warmth coating my thoughts stayed there and kept me from wondering who she was and where she was from. We lay in silence for a few minutes, the sounds of the wind the only thing I could hear. Then I let out a gasp as a cold hand splayed over my belly. It stayed there, a slight chill radiating over my skin. When I made no move to shake the hand off, it started moving in slow circles across my belly.

The simple movement relaxed me, let my muscles unclench. I stretched my arms down along my sides under the blankets and leaned into the woman next to me a little. The movement didn't stop though her fingers never warmed up. That seemed strange to me until the comforting warmth flowed over the confusion. All that was left was enjoyment. It had been so long since I'd been touched. Some time before I'd started my travels, in fact, and I'd been traveling for a while now. And she was so very beautiful.

The hand moved up from my belly, still making lazy circles, until it cupped my breast. The palm of her hand lay flat over my nipple and the pads of her fingers tapped over my heart, measuring the beat. My heart started beating faster, almost thumping against my ribcage. Her fingers followed, tapping out the quicker beat.

"Will you kiss me?" she asked, turning her head so her dark eyes met mine. "Please? It's been so long and I'm so cold."

"Yes," I replied, my voice sounding hollow in my ears. I didn't think about the fact that I didn't know her. All I wanted was to taste her lips. To kiss her as she'd asked me to do. "Yes, I will."

I propped myself up on one elbow, looking down into her eyes. All I saw was anticipation and a glittering, fierce hunger. Her fingers still tapped over my heart, keeping pace with the beat. Then I leaned down and pressed my lips to hers. Her lips were just as cold as her fingers but I barely noticed. What I did notice was that they were soft and plump, tasting faintly of peaches and vanilla. Had she had some of the same pie I'd had earlier?

Her mouth opened on a soft sigh and I didn't hesitate to taste. While I explored her mouth, with her kissing me back just as eagerly, I rested my other hand on her belly. Her skin was ice cold but I barely noticed. My fingers drew nonsense shapes on her belly as her fingers tapped out the beat of my heart. Slowly, ever so slowly, her fingers were slowing. A whispering sound started, coming from deep in her throat. I didn't wonder how that could be happening, so intent was I on kissing her. That was when I felt a tugging on the back of my throat.

The tugging was slight and, when I tried to pull back from the kiss, the warm molasses coated my thoughts again. My limbs melted, a lassitude coming over my entire body. I concentrated on kissing her again, wanting nothing more than to please her. The tugging continued and grew stronger as her fingers slowed even more over my heart. I felt a curious lightening come over me, as if I was fading. The tugging increased, like a river of air pouring from deep inside me, out through my mouth, and into hers. Her mouth was wide open now, sealed to mine in a desperate kiss. And still I didn't fight, didn't worry. I wanted this, whatever it was. I wanted her.

Everything faded away. The cold skin under my hand, the feel and taste of her lips on mine, the beat of her fingers now stilled over my heart. I felt my body vanish as the moon sank behind clouds and the icy silver light disappeared. The woman disappeared with me, a Cupid's bow shadow appearing in her place. And in my place on the bed. The smile maiden had taken my soul and made *me* a smile maiden in turn.

The shadow turned to me, the edges of the Cupid's bow turning up in a satisfied grin. The faintest shadow of a tongue swept over the bottom lip as a rumbling growl emanated from the shadow. I shivered at the sound, feeling it sweep through my shadow self, touching places that no longer existed. Then the shadow disappeared.

But I wasn't worried or afraid. I knew what I had to do now. I knew what I was. A smile maiden. So I drifted away from the room, speeding along in shadows once I was out of the building and away from the hated gleam of the fire. I shivered again, in need and desire, when I felt the warm spark of souls not far away. The moon came out from behind the clouds as I neared the souls, bathing me in its silver radiance. My shadow disappeared and my naked figure appeared, ethereal and fey limned in silver.

Please, may I join you? I'm so very cold lonely out here in the wilderness. I have missed company so, there's almost no one out here. Will you kiss me? I crave the touch of fingers, lips, and tongues. It's been so long. And I am so very hungry.

Radio Grandma
by Helen Noble

"It may feel unfair, but there's magic in the air…"

Megan removed her fingers from the "select" function of the car radio and smiled at the synchronicity; the words of a song playing on a randomly selected radio station, which just happened to reflect the very thoughts circling in her own mind. Someone, somewhere, had submitted a request for Sunday morning's Secret Songs on 102.3 Magical Moments FM. An anonymous person, who would probably never know how their choice had reached out to affirm the emotions of a complete stranger at such a poignant moment in her life. It was so unfair; her mother's life so cruelly torn away from her in such a short space of time. Megan knew that she wasn't the first person to lose her only living relative to the ravages of cancer. However, it felt as if her safety rope had been cut and she had been callously set adrift into dangerous, dark waters. It was just a short drive from the hospice where her mother, frail and weak, had finally died in her sleep just three hours previously, and for the first time in her life Megan felt completely alone, wondering how on earth she could continue to live in the world.

For the past few weeks she had been a round-the-clock visitor to the hospice, having only the company of the nurses and Pete, a man she had met on numerous occasions in the hospice cafe. He was the only visitor at his father's bedside, a constant watch, not knowing how long the vigil was to last. They had chatted in a way only two strangers confronting the death of one of their loved ones could: open, emotionally, intimately, and often with a touch of dark humour. It seemed strange to Megan that the dying should be segregated according to gender, in their last days. After all, they were all headed, in their glorious nakedness, to the same destination. However, she welcomed the brief interludes in the cafe, talking, amongst other things, about property development and interior design which momentarily distracted them both from the grim reality of their respective situations. She was always pleased to find her new companion sitting alone and his face had always lit up on seeing her.

In the early hours, the sunrise shift nurse had checked on the patient and gently roused Megan, who was dozing in the chair next to the bed, whispering that Maura had passed away. As the dawn light crept across the pristine hospice pillow, she had leaned over, casting a shadowed kiss on her mother's cold, wasted cheek for the last time. Then she had silently left the room, allowing the staff to remove the remaining intravenous equipment from her mother's child-size corpse. There had been some papers to sign in the office and Megan had returned one last time to the now-empty room to pack up her mother's few belongings, which had been left in the bedside locker.

Megan left the hospice, taking with her all the remaining traces of her mother. The next time she would see her would be in the chapel, where her body would finally be laid to rest. In her mind there seemed to be a huge, white space, a numbness that made everything else in the world feel vague and remote, until the words of the song had permeated her cold cocoon. *I'll get some sleep*, she thought to herself, on arriving home. *And then I will get on with the business of sorting out the house.*

Maura McKinley had been a feisty lady. Widowed young, with a child to raise, she had worked well into her retirement, encouraging her only daughter to get out into the world, to travel and take the chances necessary to build herself a better life. Recently, Megan's visits to her mother's house had become infrequent. She had become absorbed by the demands of her interior-design business, only learning of the advanced stage of her mother's illness, as the only next of kin, on Maura's admittance to the local hospice. Megan had travelled to be close to her mother, staying in her childhood home for the first time in five years.

Now alone, with each and every decision resting on her shoulders, Megan contemplated the fact that the family home, and its familiar contents, were her sole responsibility. The house was a three-bedroomed, 1920s semi-detached villa in a tree-lined avenue, bordering a city park in a southern suburb of London. It was here that newlyweds, Maura and Jack, had made their home amidst the optimism and relative affluence of the late 1960s, and where Megan had been born in the early 1970s. However, life for Megan and her mother changed when Jack left home one morning for work and never came back. Megan was too young to remember any of the events of the Underground tragedy when a power failure resulted in the collision of trains and the death of hundreds of people. Her father was, and always would be, the handsome, smiling, young man in the black-and-white wedding photo on the lounge wall. For Maura, life took a sharp detour and the housewife had reigned as a community-based physiotherapist so she could keep her home and raise her child. She never remarried and Megan had no memory of any male company in the house.

Grandma May moved in to help out for a while and ended up staying until the end of her days, some ten years later. As Maura settled into her retirement, keeping active by cultivating a kitchen garden and maintaining her self-reliance, Megan had become increasingly entangled in the corporate world of her career. Their lives had drifted apart; Maura's becoming more simplified and solitary, whereas Megan was constantly negotiating time limits and professional constraints, which left her little time for family or relationships. However, now a single woman in her early forties, Megan once more felt like a young girl alone in the house, just waiting for her mother to come home. Wearily, she climbed the stairs and fell asleep in her mother's bed.

On waking, Megan felt rested but still raw with the memory of her mother's death. She needed to make a list in order to help her focus and deal with all the issues in hand. However, she also needed to do something, to feel something, to somehow reassure herself that she was still alive. To sell the house as quickly as possible and get back to the city and get on with her life, Megan knew that she would have to get on with the renovation work. The place had some 1970s features which would not be great selling points – the wipe-clean wallpaper, linoleum flooring and Formica worktops in the kitchen. At least she could make a start by getting rid of this stuff.

Throwing on some old clothes that she found in her mother's wardrobe, Megan rooted around in the kitchen cupboards and the old larder, looking for some DIY tools which would help her to get started.

She would strip the walls, rip up the old carpets and arrange for the old furniture to be taken away. Then she could arrange for some workmen to come in and upgrade the kitchen units and the bathroom. Megan had an image of a house where all the clutter was cleared and the orange-and-brown floral patterns were replaced with crisp, white walls and the simple lines of functional furniture. She intended to keep it neutral to maximize selling potential. She needed to create a fresh, new space for someone else's family to occupy and call home.

It was whilst she was rummaging through the larder shelves that she came across an old transistor radio, the one her grandmother had always listened to in the kitchen when Megan, as a young girl, came home from school. Now slightly paint-splattered, and generally battered, she recalled that it had always sat on the kitchen table where she ate the warm muffins that Grandma May baked for her every afternoon. Most days, she would have to listen to the end of an afternoon Radio Four play before she was allowed to change the channel to Radio Two for some popular tunes. It was a ritual that warmed her now as she recalled those safe and comfortable times.

Megan placed the radio on the table and plugged it into the socket on the wall. *Good!* she thought to herself, it still worked. Tuning it to the frequency for receiving Radio Two, she decided that she would listen in whilst working on the kitchen, and she spent the rest of the day balancing on a stepladder and various kitchen surfaces as she removed the faded paint and curling paper of her past. In-between the sound of the steam paint stripper and electric sanding machine she caught snippets of tunes, old and new, playing on the radio as she immersed herself in the refurbishment task. Stopping for lunch, Megan realized that the music on the radio had been replaced with the sound of voices in conversation. She hadn't changed the channel, but the dial had moved and she was now listening to a Radio Four play. A strong image of Grandma May emerged from Megan's memory and, with a strange shiver she reached out for the knob and searched for more music.

The following afternoon, when Megan stepped back into the kitchen from the front door after accepting condolences from the neighbour, dear old Mrs Riley, she noticed that the station had changed once again. Feeling spooked, she hurriedly switched off the radio and sat in silence with her thoughts. Had she imagined it? Was she losing her mind? She had read somewhere that grief can sometimes have strange effects on people. Perhaps she needed to see a doctor, before the symptoms worsened and she lost her grip on reality? She brooded over a lonely dinner, a can of oxtail soup she found in the larder.

That night Megan dreamed of Grandma May. They were both in the kitchen, Grandma taking the warm muffins out of the oven and Megan, wearing her old school uniform, was sitting at the table in anticipation. She awoke feeling comforted and warm. The next day, when the radio seemed yet again to magically revert to its default setting of the afternoon play, she sat herself at the kitchen table with her paint-daubed hands wrapped around a cup of coffee, and listened.

This time she heard her Grandma's voice talking directly to her.

"Megan, now you're home, it's time we got back

down to basics!" May had always been a straight-talking sort of woman. "There are a few things you need to know before the funeral, so listen up…" Megan's trembling hands dropped the cup she was holding and reached out and snapped the radio's switch to "off." She felt as if she had been enveloped in some kind of time warp, another dimension of reality. Had she been poisoned by the paint fumes? Opening the window above the sink, she took in a deep breath of fresh air and closed her eyes. Then, feeling a little calmer, she braved the radio switch, just to reassure herself that she wasn't hallucinating any longer.

"Megan? There's no need to be afraid, child. It's me, Grandma May!" There was no doubting that voice; warm and authoritative, it had always made Megan feel safe and loved. The voice continued: "As I was saying, there are a few things we need to sort out in time for your mother's funeral. I want to make sure that everything left over there is laid to rest before she gets here."

"What do you mean?" Megan found herself saying out loud.

"There are some things your mother wanted to get done before she left but didn't have the chance to get around to doing. I promised her I would help."

"But you're dead!" Megan blurted out. "You've been gone for years!"

"Yes, but you, my dear, are alive and kicking and I promised your mother that in the space of time between her leaving there and arriving here, I would make sure that you would see to it that everything would be left just as it should be!" In a weird kind of way, this made perfect sense to Megan. Both May and Maura had been eminently practical women, both seemingly very concerned with the "how" of getting on with things, and less of the "why."

"So you've been in touch with Mum, ever since you died?" Megan's eyes were wide with incredulity.

"Of course! And so has your dad," May replied. Megan felt as if all the breath had been sucked out of her.

"Dad?" she gasped.

"Yes, Jack's right here with me now. Do you want a word?" offered the voice from the radio.

This was a just a bit too bizarre for Megan.

"Ever wondered why your mum never remarried, Meg? It was because your dad was still very much around; albeit not in a physical sense, you understand. Your grandfather's here too!"

Megan panicked, running into the hallway where she picked up the telephone to call the local clinic, booking herself an emergency doctor's appointment.

Later that evening, a rather distressed Megan found herself explaining apologetically to a registrar that she had been hearing voices and conversing with a kitchen radio, and that she thought it best to seek medical help. After filling in the Silverman Scale Questionnaire, the young doctor advised her that the depression that she appeared to be suffering was probably to be expected, given the recent death of her mother. He advised her to make a further appointment if she didn't feel any better in a couple of weeks' time, unless her symptoms worsened in the meantime, in which case she should come back straightaway.

Megan returned home with a feeling of unease. She had been reassured that she wasn't losing her mind, but she had been hearing things. She decided to submerge herself in the practicalities of the funeral arrangements, in the hope that things could return to normal as soon as possible. Tomorrow she would find out if her mother's will specified any particular funeral requirements and then she would get in touch with a local undertaker. Having completed the work in the kitchen, she moved the freestanding furniture into the hall for ease of access and arranged a collection from a local charity shop. She replaced the old transistor radio back on the larder shelf and closed the door, reasoning with herself that as soon as this business was sorted out she could get back to her own life.

It was between the early morning hours of three and four that Megan was awoken by the sound of muffled music. Mrs Riley was hard of hearing, as Megan had heard the theme tune to the old lady's favourite TV quiz through the adjoining wall in the lounge every day at five p.m. However, this didn't sound as if it was coming from next door. Making her way downstairs, Megan found that both the door to the kitchen and the door to the larder were wide open and the sound was blaring from the old transistor radio on the shelf. This was getting out of hand! She had unplugged the radio – it must be working on battery power. Megan removed the batteries and the radio fell silent. *That should do it!* she thought to herself. Confident that she wouldn't be hearing anything further from that damned radio, she took herself back to bed. But she was restless, her sleep punctuated with intrusive thoughts and images of her dead relatives.

The following morning, Megan picked up a copy of her mother's will from the family solicitors and stopped off at a local cafe to digest its contents over a creamy cappuccino. Unsurprisingly, the house and its contents were being left to her, and then there were a number of specific gifts, mainly to local charitable concerns.

"No surprises there, eh?" On hearing the words, Megan coughed out the piece of iced carrot cake that she was just about to swallow. It was her grandmother's voice, again, loud and clear.

In vain, Megan searched the other tables in the cafe, looking for, but at the same time knowing that neither she, nor anyone else, could see the source of the comment. Everyone else seemed engrossed in conversations amongst themselves; she was the only person sitting alone. What was she to do? She couldn't speak out loud to her invisible companion. She would have to just talk back in her mind.

"Can you hear me?" She heard her own voice, slow and deliberate, in her own mind.

"Of course I can!" Grandma May snapped back. "Now, can we get on with the business in hand?" Megan knew there was no escaping her now. Grandma May had connected to her brain and there was no more switching her off!

"Our generation invented the concept of wireless, if you recall," Grandma May continued. "Yours has just extended the concept to transmit other information in addition to sound."

"So you can hear my thoughts?" Megan asked silently.

"Yes."

"What, all of them, all of the time?"

"Well, it depends if I'm tuning in. Sometimes I have better things to do, you know! Although I quite agreed with you about the chap you met at the hospice. What a lovely man! And I didn't notice a wedding ring either…"

"Gran!"

Megan heard the sound of Grandma May's laughter. It had always been rather raucous and generally infectious.

"Well, what do you want me to do?" she thought to her grandmother, when the laughter subsided.

"Your mother wants you to make sure all of those financial gifts detailed in her will, the ones to Age Concern, Barnardo's and the PDSA, are distributed as soon as probate is granted on the will."

"Okay." Megan nodded her head at the empty chair opposite, and got a weird look from the woman on the next table.

"However," Grandma May continued, "in a small brown zipped case at the back of your mother's wardrobe there is some cash that she has left for you. This isn't covered in the will, and she didn't have time to write down what she wanted you to do with it. I don't think she really knew what she wanted you to do, until she went into the hospice. By then she was too weak to write down her wishes. That's why she asked me to get in contact with you."

"Are you in contact with her now?" Megan asked.

"No. We spoke just before she died, but I have to wait until she passes over before we can be in touch again."

"How come Mum never told me about you? I mean, that she talked to you?" Megan suddenly became aware that she had been sitting in silence, apparently just staring into space, for far too long now to be acceptable in a public place, and so hastily she took a slurp of her cold coffee.

"I don't know," answered Grandma May. "Perhaps she wanted you to concentrate on the future, rather than the past? Whatever the reason, I'm sure she thought she was doing the right thing. It would have been different if you had heard me yourself."

"Will I be able to hear her too, when she passes over?" Megan felt a shot of warmth in her heart at the thought.

"I don't know. I don't make the rules, but I can't see why not!" Grandma May replied.

"Okay, what does she want me to do with the money?" Megan asked, again in her mind.

"She wants you to count out two thousand pounds and donate it to the hospice where she died. It's a thank you for the kindness they showed and the comfort they allowed her in her last weeks. Oh, and she wants you to take it in person, tomorrow at exactly ten a.m." May preempted Megan's question, "Don't ask me why, just do it!"

Megan gathered herself together and returned home to look for the case and the money. True enough, just as her Grandma had described it, there was a brown leather zipped case stuffed with cash wedged behind some boxes of old photographs on the shelf at the top of the wardrobe. It was crammed full of old five and ten pound notes, a total of five thousand pounds which Megan counted out into piles of five hundred each, whilst sitting on her mother's bed. Separating two of the five thousand, she replaced the remainder in the case.

"Where did she get this money?" she asked out loud.

Grandma May replied that Maura had religiously saved something, however small, every week since Jack had died, for Megan's future. However, as Megan became more successful and independent, so her need for the money seemed to become less and so Maura had held onto it in case of an emergency. Now she had decided how she wanted her daughter to spend the money. Bemused, but also with a shiver of excitement, Megan found herself returning to the hospice. Maura's body was now in the care of the undertakers and as such, the hospice, whilst still retaining an air of familiarity, now felt much lighter to Megan. As she spoke with the ward sister, she felt a great sense of warmth and release. The tender-hearted nurse offered her a tissue and hugged her, whilst thanking her sincerely for the kind donation. As she turned to leave, Megan glanced for one last time into the cafe where she had recently spent so many hours. It was empty. Somewhere in her mind she heard a faint voice saying,

"You've missed him…" However, it was with a lighter heart that Megan left the hospice for the last time and headed home. There was just the funeral day to negotiate, and this phase of her life would be over. She could leave the house in the hands of estate agents and get back to her life in the city.

"What do you mean you've had to rearrange the funeral for a priority case? They're all dead! How can the burial of one deceased person be more important than that of another?" Megan challenged. But the undertaker stood firm by his decision and so the funeral was rescheduled for three days later than the original booking.

"Your mother will be fine with us for a few days longer, here in the chapel," he reassured her, his manner deadpan, his voice monotone.

Megan knew she would have to find something else to occupy her over the coming days and decided she would start work on redecorating the kitchen.

Initially, she had intended to employ a host of carpenters, plumbers, tilers, painters and decorators for the job. As she was still here, she thought she might as well make a start by choosing the new fitments and colour scheme. Flicking through the DIY catalogues she found herself drawn in by the detail. Instead of a neutral choice of bland colours, symmetrical shapes and standard sizes, Megan's personal tastes were overruling her professional reasoning and influencing her choice of fitments and textures. As she was measuring up for an expensive kitchen island, once again Grandma May spoke up,

"You have great taste, Megan. This kitchen is going to look amazing when it's finished! But don't spend all of your money on it. You've got a holiday to book."

"What do you mean?" Megan replied. "I have no intention of going away. As soon as this is finished, I'll be heading straight back to work."

"Listen to me," Grandma May's voice took on a more serious tone. "It's your mother's wish that you go to the travel agency and pick up a brochure. She wants you to book two weeks away to start in exactly three months' time. She said she liked the idea of you flying long-haul."

"Well, that's a bit of a tall order!" retorted Megan. "What if I don't want to fly halfway around the world on my own?"

"It's a booking for two…" came the reply.

"I must be hearing things!" Megan said out loud. "This is madness. I need to go back and talk to that doctor."

Grandma May tutted impatiently. "It's your mother's wish. It's what she wanted for you."

"How do I know? If it was written in the will, I

might not doubt my own sanity right now. But I only have your word for it, and how do I even know if you are who you say you are, and that this whole thing is not just a symptom of my sick mind?" Megan was beginning to panic. Was she going mad? What would people think if they looked through the window and could see her talking out loud to herself? She rummaged around in her bag for the number of the local clinic, with the intention of calling for a further appointment with the doctor. She was stilled by the sound of her father's voice.

"Megan, it's me, Dad."

Her grieving heart lurched. It had been so many years since she had heard his voice, yet instantly it felt as if she was a small child again, safe in his arms.

"Your mother only wanted what was best for you. We all want what's best for you, so please don't think this is about anything other than that."

"Dad?" whispered Megan. "Dad, is this real?"

"Yes," the calm voice replied. "We're all here, waiting for your mother to arrive. What you are being asked to do, just know that it's all for a good reason. Darling, we love you and we just want you to be happy." A trail of tears pooled softly into the dark circles under Megan's eyes before silently dripping down her cheeks. She felt so very tired. The tragic events of the past few weeks were now starting to take their toll on her emotional reserves. Her feelings were raw. She wanted to curl up under the protective cover of sleep and simply drift off to be with her family. But those on the other side had different ideas.

"Megan, just book the holiday. What harm can it possibly do?" Her Dad's voice was low and hypnotic. *He's right,* thought Megan. *It's only money. So what if I don't even make the flight?* It wasn't as if she would be causing harm to anyone else. After all, there was just her, now...

"*Fourteen nights, island hopping around the stunning ten-island archipelago that is Cape Verde... we will fly you to the top of the Pico de Fogo volcano and drop you into the verdant valleys of Santo Antao. You can explore the bustling markets at Santiago and bliss out on the golden beaches at Sal,*" read Megan. Inspired by the scenery in the brochure she tried working out the cost, including the sale price discount. However, a booking scheduled for the end of November would still prove too expensive if she booked for two. Perhaps this wasn't the holiday for her? She closed the glossy brochure and rested her exhausted head in her hands on the kitchen table.

As the funeral approached, the radio remained respectfully silent in the house. Megan washed, dried and ironed her clothes, hanging them on the outside of the wardrobe in readiness for the service. The solitary funeral car was booked to arrive at ten thirty a.m. to take her firstly to the service at the Chapel of Rest, before moving on to the crematorium. The idea of booking a car just for herself had seemed ludicrous, and so she had invited Mrs Riley to accompany her. There would be some surviving associates of her mother at the service. However, Megan knew she would not be surrounded by friends and family. As she helped the friendly widow into the second row of the polished black seven-seater car, Megan felt grateful for her company, acutely aware of how alone she was in the world. Being hard of hearing, Mrs Riley attempted only the merest of conversational pleasantries during the journey, seemingly content to hold Megan's hand firmly within the grasp of her own. But the silence was not to last for long. Megan soon sensed some disturbance in the third row of seats, behind herself and Mrs Riley. Then she heard them: the voices, they were back. Amidst a general sense of jostling, she quite clearly heard Grandma May's voice:

"I think it should be me, after all she is my daughter. You men can keep each other company outside."

What on earth...? Megan had the uneasy feeling that her deceased relatives would be attending the funeral. *How bizarre!* The voices quietened. However, as the car approached the crematorium, Megan once again sensed an uneasy atmosphere.

"Yes, I'm going to do it now, as she steps out of the car," said her grandmother's voice. And as she leaned over to help her elderly companion out of the car, Megan felt what could only be described as a deep but gentle penetration, a surge of energy that touched the core of her being. Whilst not unpleasant, it was very unsettling and, as she straightened up, Megan felt faint. The colour drained from her cheeks and she steadied herself with her hand against the roof of the car.

"Are you all right, dear?" Mrs Riley asked, most concerned. "You look as if you've seen a ghost!"

Regaining her balance, Megan took a deep breath and reassured her companion that she was fine.

"It's time to go inside," she said, softly.

Taking their seats at the front of the chapel, the two women stared at the coffin laid out before them. Megan could hear the hushed movements of others entering the building from behind, but she kept her focus firmly in front of her. However, she was struggling to sit still. Strange waves of strange energy were washing over her, and for a moment or two, she felt as if her body was moving independently of her mind. Then she felt it: a great big sigh of relief, emanating from low in her abdomen and inflating her chest.

"Ah! It feels so good to be embodied once more," announced Grandma May in a muffled tone. Frantic, Megan looked around. No one else seemed to have heard the voice.

"Where are you?" Megan asked with her thoughts, fearing that she already knew the answer.

"I'm inside you," whispered Grandma May, as the hum in the room quietened and the service commenced. Megan's mind was in a whirl. Although her body was present in the room, her thoughts were spiraling into unknown territory. She could not deny the sensation of her grandmother's spirit within her and, as a result, her own mind had become open to a myriad of possibilities. She smiled apologetically as her grandmother insisted on using her eyes to stare intently at the face of every person in the room, commenting on how well, old, or ill they were looking.

A closer gathering at the crematorium enabled Megan to listen a little more closely to the internal dialogue between her mother and grandmother. May then announced to her granddaughter that she would soon be leaving her body, to accompany Maura in her passing over into the spirit world. As the curtain closed on the flower-clad coffin, she heard the reassuring words of Grandma May to her daughter:

"Welcome home, my darling Maura. We are so pleased you are finally here with us."

"Thank you, it feels so good to arrive," Maura replied.

Feeling the sensation of the spirit of Grandma May leaving her body and hearing her mother's voice, Megan wept. The rest of the afternoon remained something of a blur in her memory; however, she recalled one event. It was through her tears that she saw the face of Pete, the man from the hospice, as their respective funeral cars crossed paths at the entrance gate to the crematorium.

Three days later, Megan awoke in the cold, lonely house with a mission in mind. Rifling through the week's mail which had gathered on the welcome mat at the front door, she found a flyer advertising the services of a local building contractor. Leaving a message on the voicemail of the mobile number on the page, she requested a call back explaining the possible opportunity for a house renovation project. *Who knows? Perhaps he might even want to buy the house*, she mused. Next, she telephoned the travel agent and, using her credit card, booked a two-week holiday to the Cape Verde islands. She decided that she would use the stash of cash left by her mother to pay the balance in six weeks' time.

Three Months Later

"Well, you could have given us a bit more notice," huffed Grandma May inside Megan's mind as she excitedly unzipped her bulging suitcase on the king size bed in the luxurious hotel room.

"You didn't have to come!" Megan retorted.

"What? You, our only living relative, finally getting married, and you don't think we want to attend?" Megan knew by the old lady's tone that the spirits were secretly pleased.

"Well, you were so insistent that we met," laughed Megan, as she lifted a silky shift from the case. She held it up against the bright light streaming in through the hotel window, which revealed a sparkling azure sea set against the breathtaking backdrop of a volcanic mountain.

"Yes, and even with our help you couldn't get it right!" Grandma May laughed. "He left the hospice before you arrived to make the donation, and then the funeral car had to take a detour and so your paths failed to cross at the crematorium."

"So you had a hand in the rescheduling of the funeral?" Megan asked.

"I'm afraid so," answered Grandma May, a little subdued. "We try not to interfere, but sometimes…"

"And you orchestrated the flyer in the mail?" Megan was getting a fuller picture.

"Yes! We had a word, and as soon as he picked up the voicemail message he experienced an urgency to pay you a visit. We are pleased about your plans for the house. It will make a great first home for you two, together."

Sensing that something was happening in the bedroom, the subject of the conversation stepped out of the en-suite bathroom. "This is amazing!" he exclaimed. "How did you find this place?"

"I had quite a lot of guidance," laughed Megan. "I think we're going to enjoy it here. It's the perfect place for the start of our life together."

"Let's start now…" There was a twinkle in Pete's eyes as he gently steered her by the shoulders towards the bed.

"The wedding ceremony isn't for another three days," piped up Grandma May.

"You spirits don't get to make all the decisions for the living," Megan replied with her thoughts. "And now might be a good time for you to tune out…"

THE DURGA
BY L. S. REINHOLT

```
Name: Rohin Latch
Age: 48 TY
Rank: Captain
Vessel: The Aditi - commercial
    freighter - Amaltean Trade
    Fleet
Status: en route to Procyon Colony
    IX - 3 years out
```

Rohin straightened up in her chair, stretched and groaned. She really should not have let herself drift off at the helm. She wasn't young anymore and neither her back nor her neck would forgive her soon for the cramped position. And her cabin was so close. She could have been lying comfortably in her bed and might actually have felt rested now, rather than bordering on miserable.

Luckily she had learned from past mistakes. Yawning, she reached out for the small disk resting on top of the console, pressed it to the skin just below her ear and let it release a strong, numbing agent into her blood.

A minute later, she was able to get to her feet without too much discomfort. She made it all the way to her cabin door before she realised what had woken her in the first place.

The faint peep repeated itself every ten seconds and had probably been going for a good five minutes before she'd stirred. She had been meaning to adjust the volume, but she got so few messages during flight that it had never really been an issue before.

And it was never anything urgent anyway. Once the Aditi had reached cruising velocity, there really wasn't much call for any kind of communication for the duration of the voyage. Not before the start of deceleration would she receive confirmation of the order that had sent her out here in the first place.

Getting a message at this point did not bode well. With an average travel time of five years, a lot could change during the voyage and it was not uncommon for a colony to cancel a trade before the ship could arrive. On one occasion the colony itself had been withdrawn.

Rohin had made three journeys now, from Amaltea to Proxima, then on to Luyten and from there to Procyon. Unless another order was waiting for her there, she would head back to Sol, where she'd have accumulated two decades' worth of a captain's salary. With interest. More than enough to see her comfortably settled. If that was what she chose.

But if this message was to tell her that the delivery to the colony in the Procyon system had been cancelled, she would have to turn around and head for another system, losing years of travelling as well as fifty per cent of the fee. Then the heavens only knew when she'd be able to retire.

Not sure what she was hoping for, Rohin opened the message. It was not from Procyon. Or Amaltea.

```
***This is an automated distress signal from the
  colony ship Durga, destination Procyon IV***
```

Rohin read the message again, then requested a scan of the frequency on which it had been received. There was nothing else. What was the point of a distress signal that did not state the nature of the emergency? Nor the location of the vessel?

She was sorely tempted to ignore it, but the Aditi had already logged the message and if she did not make at least a token effort to assist the Durga, the penalty would be quite severe, depending on who was in power by the time she reached Procyon.

So she programmed a trace of the signal and, figuring it could take hours, made her way to the small bathroom at the back of her cabin for a long, lukewarm shower.

Returning to the helm, she confirmed that the search was still not complete, picked up a small meal pack and returned to her cabin.

A loud buzz announced that the search was finished. Rohin paused the show she had been watching on the screen above her bunk, pushed the image to the corner and called up the results.

It seemed the ship had been parked in orbit around a small rogue moon, not too far off her course. She'd lose only a month diverting there. Assuming, of course, that the emergency could be dealt with quickly.

Most likely scenario was that the ship and its crew were already dead and all she would be able to do is retrieve the log and file a report. If there were any survivors, she would have to bring them on board and though it would be highly inconvenient, the Aditi was adequately equipped to carry a significant number of passengers for the remainder of the voyage.

With a heavy sigh she pushed herself off her bunk and headed for the bridge to make the necessary adjustments. Just as expected, her neck and lower back were starting to feel stiff and she once again cursed her unfortunate habit.

The two weeks passed by as any other she had spent on the ship. She ate, slept, read or watched stories on the screens and checked the systems three times a day. She also did look up the Durga in the records, but, as expected, the information was rather sparse. It was a standard colony ship carrying a crew of seven, as well as thirty-five passengers and the supplies needed to start a new colony on an already settled planet.

The planned colony was registered as collectivistic and the colonists had, as was often seen in such groups, twice as many women as men. This, of course, made sense from a reproductive perspective, but was also generally considered preferable for socioeconomic reasons that Rohin had never quite understood.

Nothing about the Durga seemed unusual. Except for the fact that it had apparently gone slightly off course. And that it was not responding to any of the messages she had sent, informing the crew that help was on its way.

And yet, she found, as the Aditi slowed down to match the orbit of the Durga, the ship appeared completely unharmed. Its external sensors were still working and, scanning it, she found that the engines were still on. It was not the wreck she had expected. Just a parked ship. Devoid of all life.

She donned her suit, just in case, and made her way to the airlock, arriving mere seconds after the two ships connected. The atmosphere should be stable on the other ship, but just in case, she put on her helmet as the heavy latch swung open.

The room she entered was almost identical to the

one she'd left, except for the panel by the door which looked to be a more recent model. Most ships of the major Terran fleets were produced by the same conglomerate of manufacturers, so this was no surprise. Neither was the design of the corridor that she followed to the bridge nor the faint orange tinted light. Someone must have switched off the circadian simulator, or the ship would have been in daytime mode.

She considered cancelling this order, but decided against it. The emergency light was sufficient and as long as she did not know what had happened, it was best not to disturb anything.

Sitting in the captain's chair, she ran a routine check of the system. Everything was working and the air, though slightly stale, was as it should be. She still held her breath for a moment as she removed her helmet, then laughed at herself.

Rohin called up the ship's log and began reading. The first years of the voyage had gone as planned. There had been some unrest between a few of the colonists. And two nuptials, both performed by the captain. And then, three months ago, there was a brief entry about an anomaly followed by a change in course and estimated time of arrival. And then... nothing.

Rohin checked twice. The log had just stopped. A whole week before the Durga had reached its current location.

She sat there for a long time, thinking. Then with a sigh she got up, removed the outer layer of her suit and set off to explore the ship.

It was almost twice as large as the Aditi, with half the space taken up by living quarters, mess hall and recreational areas. The rest was divided between the engine, recycling systems and storage.

She started with the crew's cabins and then moved on to the passengers'. All were the same. All were empty.

The bunks and other furniture were still there, but no clothes, toiletries, or any other sign that these rooms had ever been inhabited.

Had the ship been taken? Or had the colonists packed their belongings and left? And if so, where had they gone?

There were so many questions on the Durga. And no answers.

No answers, that is, until she reached the lowest level of the cargo stalls.

At first, Rohin did not know what she was looking at. If there even was a "what" to be seen. But she could feel it. As she moved closer, her skin tingled and she caught a fleeting hint of a vaguely familiar smell. The air felt slightly cooler in that particular corridor. Cooler and drier.

The thing itself was the exact same size and shape as every doorway on the ship. But it was standing freely in the air, neither touching the floor nor the ceiling. And it was transparent.

Well, not really transparent. Because as far as she could tell, there was nothing there to see through. Just a field of air that shimmered and undulated whenever she approached it and then grew still as she withdrew.

It was fascinating and strangely beautiful. She spent close to an hour observing and interacting with it before she thought to return to the bridge for a scan. Surely such an optical effect would require some kind of tech. Something that was not standard equipment for a colony ship. Or any kind of ship that she knew of.

Back on the bridge, she took control of the computer and proceeded to perform every type of scan possible. With no result. She programmed the main monitor to show the corridor, finding that the phenomenon did not even show up on the screen. She flicked through all the settings but the corridor appeared empty.

How could that be? Had it disappeared while she was doing the scans?

She practically ran down to the corridor, gasping in relief as the phenomenon began to sparkle and ripple.

She walked right up to it, holding her palm only an inch from its nonexistent surface. What was it? Where had it come from? And why?

Questions, questions and more questions. That was all she found as she searched the ship again, went over every entry of the main and the technical log made two months back from the diversion, and spent hour after hour watching the thing.

She had planned to return to the Aditi for meals and rest. But when she was finally overcome by fatigue, she only managed to make her way to the nearest cabin on the Durga. Upon waking, she returned to the Aditi for a meal and shower.

As soon as she entered her own ship, she felt restless. And, when she headed back to the Durga, she brought along food and water for a prolonged stay.

On the third day she finally had a breakthrough. She had been staring at the thing for ten hours and it had done nothing except react whenever she reached a hand towards it. In frustration, she chucked an empty water bottle at it and then jumped to her feet as there was a loud snap and the bottle disappeared.

A portal! It was a portal of some kind.

She threw a few more objects at it, all with the same result, then fetched a long metal rod and tried poking it through. It didn't work. The rod just passed straight through the rippling field as if it was nothing but air. She could even tap the walls of the corridor with it.

She pulled it back and examined it. It was completely unchanged.

She tried again, and when the rod was halfway through the portal, she let go of it.

It disappeared.

Rohin returned to the bridge, this time to search through much older records, not about the travels of the Durga or Aditi, but regarding observations reported by the first explorers who ventured beyond the Sol system. Surely someone must have encountered something similar to the portal before.

There were a lot of theories about wormholes and ripples, but nothing concrete. No one had ever seen such a thing. And none of the theories she could find seemed to apply to this particular phenomenon.

Finally she gave up figuring out what it was. Instead, she began speculating how and why the crews and passengers of the Durga had disappeared. They must have gone through the portal, but under what circumstances?

Had they been forced? No, there would be signs of combat if that were so. Casualties left behind. Perhaps they were lured then? Persuaded via mind control? There were rumours that such abilities were being stimulated and researched at unlicensed laboratories in the remote colonies.

Rohin soon dismissed this idea. Not that she would put it past some of these self-proclaimed scientists to attempt such a thing, but because she doubted any of them could have discovered both the way to control the minds of more than forty people as well as the technology to create the portal.

No, it was definitely not Terran.

So it had to be alien. It seemed the only logical explanation. But not plausible.

In the centuries since humanity had first ventured beyond their own solar system, they had not yet encountered even a hint of other intelligent life. Plenty of bacteria and single cell organisms. Even a few creatures resembling Terran invertebrates. But nothing complex. Nothing sentient.

Until now. Because the portal could not be a natural phenomenon. Someone must have made it. Made it and placed it here.

And the Durga had found it. Must have been drawn to it somehow, since they had gone off their designated course to come to it.

Had the portal sent out some sort of signal? Why had nothing been mentioned about it in the ship's logs? Why had nothing been left behind?

The questions swarmed in her head. Questions that could not possibly be answered with so little tangible information.

Rohin ran through the empty ship, tearing panels from the walls and overturning furniture. There must be something. Anything! Anything that could give her just some kind of clue. She had to know. She had to know what had happened to the crew, the passengers. Why they had gone through the portal.

They must have learned *something*. What was it? Who had made it? Where did it lead? They would not have gone through without knowing these things. Had they sent someone ahead? Someone to report back to let them know that it was safe? That would be the sensible thing to do, and Rohin had almost convinced herself that this must have been the case, when she realised something:

If it was possible to pass both ways through the portal, why had no one returned? If nothing else, to leave a message to whomever would find the ship. They could have sent a message to Procyon. Or back to Terra. They could have left a piece of paper on the bridge or even scribbled something on the wall of the cargo stall.

But there was nothing. She had gone over the ship too many times to have missed such a message.

They must all have gone through, not knowing what was waiting on the other side. Why? Why take such a risk? What were they hoping to find?

Rohin ended up back on the lowest level of the cargo stalls. Sitting on the floor, just watching the air where the portal was hidden. She could sense it now. Not with her eyes or ears. Not even the faint scent she had noticed earlier. She couldn't explain it, she just... she just felt it. Right there. Waiting.

But she would not wait any longer. There were no answers to be found here. She might as well not have come.

It was time to return to the Aditi. Time to move on.

```
***This is an automated distress signal from the
   cargo ship Aditi, destination Procyon IX***
```

WARREN WOMB
BY ALEX CLARKE

Lay. Waiting. Soon to be vindicated. Certain the nurse would find the large Grey Hare, not cancer. That was the only reason she was here, legs akimbo, labia shaved. Not too much. She did not want to enter the "sleek whore" territory as her mother had put it. Just a tidy up. Neat enough to uphold the lie that she voted progressively in elections, enjoyed being a member of the PTA, and didn't take dodgy sleeping pills bought online. Bushy but neat. Shaggy but tidy. Animal infested, but clean.

"Deep breath in," said the nurse with the heavy, red hands.

She complied. Cold sharp expanding pressure – vagina prised open.

"Just going to look at your cervix first."

Look into the moon's eye you mean, she thought as her head spun and heart tripped jazz.

Dimwit breathe, came her father's words, hiding beneath the cape of her own voice. Familiar enemies become friends with time. Invited into warm chairs by the mind's fire. Offered a drink, cigar, and told stories. Sometimes secrets.

The Hare had appeared one night. With vague disinterest she estimated the event took place about a month before. Under a full moon. Big Hammer Horror full moon. Beaming shining inviting smiling. Early autumn. Wasps were humming looking for winter homes. She kept the windows shut, afraid. Protecting her sugar jar from spite. *Wasps kill bees*, her father had told her, *with no God-given reason either.* She had wondered what a God-given right would look like. A deed? A Certificate? A small card you keep in your wallet? Sad wind bullied with indiscriminate hate. Deaf, blind, dumb to reason. Trees suffered the most. Crumpled with despair, leaves lost the will. She kept the curtains drawn. Blocking natural expressions of throttling violence. Avoiding trips to the shops that required shuffling through the departed leaves. They say trees don't die, they fall asleep. *So leaves aren't trees*, she'd thought as a child, they're just bits of trees. Like hair or nails. Cells. Wasps out, chaos blocked by curtains. While making pots of tea she'd pondered mercy. What it was. How it was sought. Who owned it? It was then she had decided to start taking sleeping pills during the day. To hibernate. Dates merged. Twenty-first of something or other…

"Everything looks fine," said the nurse without a smile. "We'll proceed."

She saw the nurse lift something long. Snapping her eyes shut, she turned her face to the wall. Not fast enough to show she was afraid, a small enough movement to maintain dignity. She held her breath.

The moon had been full. Hammer Horror full. Rising with ease over her house. She lay on the bed, watching the Hammer Horror full moon rise above her. She could see it through the wall, the ceiling, and the roof above. She could feel it call to the water within her, feel the water's rolling desire to ascend. Pulling against her skin towards the dead sky rock. Her moisture wanted to become the sea of tranquillity. Yet, everything within burned. Ghosts. Droplet phantoms. Water demons. All bubbled beneath the dermis, trapped. Angry. Bubbling rage. Pushing. Urging her skin to split in their desperate search for cold heaven. She had screamed from somewhere far back in her throat. A hidden place that caught the sound and inverted its vibrational trajectory backwards. She felt her heart would pop with the pressure. Hammer Horror full moon hung in the sky watching. Then it blinked. Blinked and blobbed apart like the innards of a lava lamp. Blob. Two moon eyes. Blinking. Then around them, the clouds danced to form a giant grey hare's face. The moon-eyed Grey Hare looked down at her with crater encrusted irises. Glinting. Blinking.

"You'll feel a scraping."

She let out her breath and quickly took another deep lungful.

"Just breathe normally."

Early autumn, wasps locked out, sad wind blowing, lay in bed, water ascending, Hammer Horror full moon revealed as crater encrusted moon-eyed giant Grey Hare. Mesmerised by the dead depth of white within Grey Hare's eyes she barely noticed the ghosts, droplet phantoms, water demons break free from her pores to rise, rise, rise with silent, slow grace, upwards towards Grey Hare's magnificent beaming dead eyes. Heaven. Peace. Quiet. Unseen, unspoken, release. Grey Hare moved her face away. Clouds parted, her face disintegrated, her moon eyes merged together. Hammer Horror full moon gleamed, disinterested once more. She had tried to raise a hand to wave goodbye to her stellar friend, when strength failed. *Goodbye* whispered from within her own mind. When simultaneously *Hello* resounded in stereo around her. *Hello* said a smaller Grey Hare who emerged from Hammer Horror full moon and bounded through the sky towards her. Bold, proud, visible, happy, excited, it leapt towards her, through the roof, through the ceiling, breaking into the room with an explosion of wild rampant lavender and straight up her vagina.

"Nearly done."

Early autumn panic. Beneath a Hammer Horror full moon panic. The Grey Hare bounced through her inner space with a joy she had never known. Panic. Terror forced silent contortion. Her panic-stricken fingers searched her vagina, her breath stole her voice. Burrowing. The Grey Hare was burrowing. She could feel its feet by her ovaries. Still Grey Hare burrowed further. Large clownish feet scraping in her inner earth. Each turn of its body kicking up hell; loneliness, sadness, despair. Three dimensional space. She felt wide, expansive, alive, growing. The Grey Hare ran with joy within her spaces. Her fingers pursued the creature. Within, without notification nor warning, Grey Hare's feet began stamping out stars. Big small tickly itchy stars. Leap happy leap, sweeping twirl, leap happy leap! Stars became constellations. Electrified sound broke from within her throat. Her fingers stopped their frenzied wandering. Sound. Deep sound, heavy sound, big sound. Low, loud sound bounded unabashed from her throat and knocked the lamp off the bedstead. Fast tired rapture broke within her body. All was light. All danced. All was forgotten, forgiven, and redeemed.

"All done."

"Well?"

"Well, your cervix looks healthy from what I can see. We'll send off the rest and you'll know next week."

Desperation. She stood naked from the waist down unsure what to say.

"Don't worry."

"But–"

"Listen, at your age the chances of cancer are very slim."

"No I mean–"

"You've only skipped one period, and your symptoms are minimal."

She wondered if she could ask the nurse to check again. How do you miss a hare?

"It's probably stress that's done it."

"Done what?" she asked, strange desolation threatening to throttle her sense of self.

"Your missed period."

The strange feeling of desolation punched her in the heart.

"I'm not stressed."

"How are you sleeping?"

"Fine, fine." She pulled on her jeans.

"Great, ok. You'll hear next week then."

Great, ok. I'll hear next week, she repeated. Her feet, feeling fragile, bruised, pressed the floor as she left the room, the building and into the street beyond. *Just a week,* she thought, *I can do this.*

The furry grey head within her concurred with a nod.

QUEEN OF THE ANIMALS
BY GEMMA CARTMELL

The day Elis witnessed the death of a chimney sweep, he was walking across the bridge leading from the fields where firewood was collected, back towards the archway into town. Winter seemed eternal to the townsfolk as it snowed most of the year. Today the snow was thick on the ground. In his hands Elis carried logs to warm the fire for his mother and father. As he sung a light melody in his head, he looked down at the stream below him. It was frozen solid, a blanket of ice. He hoped the local children would be careful when playing down there.

Halfway across the bridge he heard the sound of an animal in pain. He looked to his right where a footpath followed the stream. All he could see was one of the local chimney sweeps, on his knees by the stream. He seemed to be pulling something out of a hole in the ice.

Elis heard the animal again, growling in terror, and without hesitation dropped the logs and raced the rest of the way across the bridge and down the path towards the man. He only stopped when he saw the animal in the netted trap.

It was a snow tiger. Its face was scrunched up and its mouth was open in rage, revealing its gleaming white teeth. Its white coat, having once been beautiful and lush, had stains of red where the deadly barbs stabbed, invented to hurt these creatures and nothing else. The tiger growled furiously, attempting to pull away from the man as he heaved it onto the footpath. Its legs were unable to move from the net's grip.

"Disgusting creature," Elis heard the man grumble under his breath. "Disgusting. You shouldn't be here, scaring the poor children."

Elis sensed the creature's pain. No one in the town cared much for animals, especially not ones as dangerous as this. Most were killed on sight. But Elis was different. Seeing the tiger's blood smear across the snowy ground angered him. He took out his small knife which he used for cutting wood for the fire and stormed towards the chimney sweep, breaking into a run.

"Stop!" he yelled. "Let the creature go!"

The man turned and put out a hand for Elis to stay away. "Don't tell me what to do," he said. "You stay there while I finish the job."

Before Elis could speak his attention was caught by the snow tiger. Its eyes snapped open, staring straight at him. The eyes were incredible – an icy purple. Very slowly Elis took a step back; something was happening to the tiger, something only one person could do. The blood on the tiger's white coat was fading a bit at a time, the wounds healing rapidly, miraculously. Elis almost dropped his knife and quickly returned it to its sheath. He watched in awe as a new kind of strength was unleashed into this beautiful creature.

The snow tiger roared.

"What the–?" the man cried. "What are you – No! Not her! Not her!"

The Queen, Elis thought, and his astonishment was replaced by fear. He stepped back. "Good sir!" he cried to the man. "You must let him go, before it's too late!"

The man didn't seem to hear and instead tried to restrain the tiger by pulling at the net. However, as

Elis predicted, the net was now useless and slipped from the tiger as easily as a necklace from one's own neck. The man still held onto the net with shock on his face. He had no time to run.

"No!" Elis yelled as the tiger leapt onto the chimney sweep. Though the white fur had been rid of blood, in moments red coated it afresh. The tiger went for the man's chest and, as it raised its head, the man's heart hung in shreds from its blood-splattered jaws.

Elis's stomach turned. He had no strength to stop this animal. There was no point now, no point in stopping it if the deed had been done.

The tiger dropped the heart and looked up at Elis. He backed away, putting up a hand. He flinched as the tiger ran towards him. But it only raced past him, through the main archway into town. Screams erupted from within and Elis raced through the archway himself.

The snow tiger paid no heed to the townsfolk. It headed north towards its home, the white stone castle set in the mountain beyond the town. As cold as the castle looked, Elis knew there was life within it. Birds flew across its tallest towers, where many more animals surely rested. For it was the Queen's castle, and she was their protector.

That night, Elis cooked dinner for his family. His parents and darling little brother, Tim, had been shocked to hear about the death of the chimney sweep. The body had been taken by the townsfolk and buried in the woods. Elis had gone to give his condolences to the chimney sweep's family and ventured back shortly afterwards. He hadn't wanted to hang around. He was glad to be back in his cosy house, with the ones he loved.

He crouched by the log fire, stirring a hot pot of vegetable soup. It smelled good. Behind him, his parents sat in their usual seats, his mother knitting and his father resting his eyes.

Tim sat on the floor by Elis, watching him stir. He was nine years old with rich brown hair and blue eyes like gems. He was rather intelligent for his age; a real thinker, a real adventurer. Elis knew Tim would grow to be stronger than he himself was. Even now he demonstrated great strength.

Elis got his blond hair and pale blue eyes from his mother. He believed he had more traits from his mother than father, though he had a sense of curiosity which she didn't possess.

Soon the family were sitting at the dining table, tucking into their soup. Elis gave his little brother a roll he'd bought from the bakery that morning, and the two of them shared it beneath the table.

"So!" their father bellowed. He wiped his mouth with his napkin and carried on. "A snow tiger! Another of the Queen's pets?"

Elis put down his spoon and glanced at Tim, whose soft eyes were waiting for a reply. He sighed in defeat.

"I'm very certain it was one of the Queen's, yes," he replied. "I doubt she meant it to hurt anyone, though. By healing it she was only protecting it from harm."

"Hmm," Elis's father grumbled. "The Queen of the Animals, heh. A fine name she's given herself. It's as if she cares for her dangerous predators more than her own people.'

"Of course she doesn't. But the Queen sees the animals as people, too. She had to do something.

Wouldn't you be upset, Father, if one of your sons got caught up in a net, weak and unable to fight back? Wouldn't you do anything to save us?"

"I wouldn't kill an innocent person, no."

"Innocent isn't exactly the word to describe that man, Father."

Elis's father grunted under his breath, avoiding eye contact with Elis. Tim and their mother tried to smile at Elis but their smiles only faded.

Nothing more was said. Elis cleared the table and his father sulked his way off to bed. Elis's mother asked if he would be kind enough to tuck Tim in, so he led Tim by the hand up to the small attic bedroom which they shared. There they got into their nightgowns and Elis drew the blankets from Tim's bed, tucking him in tight and kissing his cheek.

"The Queen has no evil in her," Elis whispered. "I know it."

"Why did she let the tiger hurt that man?" Tim asked, his face peeking out from under the covers. His eyes were scared, and Elis kissed him again to reassure him.

"You have nothing to fear," Elis answered. "She is a strong queen, and she has a power many fear. But in my eyes it is a beautiful power, one that we all should rejoice in. It is a blessing to be able to communicate with animals, to lend them strength. She treats them as family, and rightfully so. Animals are just as important as human beings. The chimney sweep hurt a member of the Queen's family, therefore he was punished."

"She just wanted to save her family?" Tim asked.

Elis nodded. "But Father has a point. No man should have been killed because of this."

"What are you going to do about it?"

Elis smiled mysteriously. He had a plan. He had been thinking of it all night. Suddenly he felt his nerves creep up on him. Was he brave enough?

"I will wait until dawn," he said. "Then I shall see about meeting our queen. She does not accept audiences but if she understands that I respect her, she might make an exception. We'll have to see. For now, we must sleep. Tomorrow is a new day."

The next morning Elis woke early. Those who knew about yesterday's tragedy glanced at him as he passed through town. The streets narrowed as he made his way up towards the castle, and the glances grew more suspicious. Unlike the rest of the townsfolk, he respected the Queen and her animals, and they distrusted him for it. And now here he was, the very day after a man was killed by one of the Queen's own snow tigers, making his way towards her castle. He wondered what they must think of him.

Snow began to fall. The flakes were so big Elis could make out the crystals in each. Moving through the crowd, a man sneezed from the cold.

The houses stopped a fair distance away from the castle's white gates. The gates were unguarded, yet still managed to look ominous. Behind them lay the castle's main doors, carved into the rock of the mountain. Elis looked up. Fifty feet above, the castle loomed over him. He shut his eyes and forced himself to be strong. As he opened them again, he let his feet carry him to the front gates. He placed his naked hands against them and tried to push them open. They would not budge.

With a sigh, Elis took a step back. Just as he was thinking of climbing over, two shadows appeared to his right. He turned and saw two beautiful robins. They flew to sit on top of the gate. Both fixed their gazes on Elis.

Elis licked his lips, gulped, and then knelt on one knee. He bowed his head to the robins.

"I'm here to see the Queen," he said to them. "I'm not here to harm her. I just want to speak with her."

The robins blinked at the same time and ruffled their wings, as if they were laughing. They didn't move from their spot but, with a click, the gates creaked open.

Elis stood up. He nodded gratefully to the robins before hurrying on. Beyond the gates was a garden with patches of grass covered in snow. There were some chairs and a swing, which the Queen supposedly used, but Elis hadn't ever heard of her coming out here to relax. No one had seen her face in years.

Elis was surprised when he tried the main doors, for they were unlocked. Chills rushed down his spine and he held his head high before opening the door fully and stepping inside the Queen's own castle.

The entire room was white. The light coming from the walls, floor and ceiling cast a bright glow. Elis felt as if he had entered Heaven itself. The room was empty apart from a white throne at the back wall, which he could barely see, so profound was the whiteness of the room.

Elis startled upon noticing a vase of brightly coloured roses sat upon a white table next to the main doors. The roses were different shades of purple and blue. It was strange seeing something so vibrant in such an empty room. He crept his way towards the table and inspected the roses.

The flap of wings made him look up and he took a step back as a flock of white doves glided down towards him. Each had a rose in its beak and one by one they placed them in the vase. Then they flew away again, upwards. Elis watched them go and realised the ceiling seemed eternal; he could not see where it ended. He turned his attention back to the flowers and lightly touched a purple rose. He leant towards it and smelled it. The intense aroma was incredible, as if the flower had been drowned in perfume.

I must be dreaming, Elis thought. *All this cannot be real.*

He stepped away from the vase of flowers, back to the open space of white. He had to ascend to meet the Queen. That was his hunch.

Near the throne he spotted an archway that led to another room. He ran to it, impatient, and raced through into a smaller room where a small spiral staircase ascended. In the corner of this room was another vase full of roses.

He took the stairs two at a time. There was no telling as to how high up he was once he reached the top. He panted for a moment, back bent, before inspecting the space surrounding him. He was confronted by a fawn. She trotted over to him and gazed at him like the robins had done. Elis bowed his head to her.

"I'm here to see the Queen," he said again. "I'm not here to harm her. I just want to speak with her."

The fawn tilted her head to one side before walking towards the double doors across the room. Elis followed her. Like in the other rooms, there were roses in white vases by the doors.

Elis and the fawn stood, glanced at one another,

and then Elis entered the room with the fawn following behind.

As soon as he opened the door, Elis stopped in his tracks.

In the middle of the room was the Queen. She sat on a throne with her animals around her. She wore a purple dress with light pink and blue flowers draped over it in chains. She was pale, with a touch of pink in her cheeks and lips. There was a coldness to her eyes. They were blue, almost purple, and Elis found them striking to look at. There was no crown on her head but flowers were woven through her long black hair; a purple rose was amongst them. Woodland animals huddled by her feet, and birds sat across her throne and on her shoulders. In her arms a grey rabbit lay, stroked by a delicate hand. On either side of her were a couple of stags.

Slowly Elis stepped forward. The animals watched him. They did not seem afraid. They were like a living shield, keeping him from the Queen. He knelt on one knee and bowed.

"My Lady," he said. "I'm grateful you've allowed me this audience." He lifted his head but stayed knelt. "I'm here to bring peace to our town."

Up close, Elis noticed just how young she looked. Around his age, maybe younger. She had a mature aura, though, that had little to do with her simply being a queen. Her mouth opened but she didn't utter a word at first. Her expression grew serious and weary.

"What is your name?" she asked.

"My name is Elis, My Lady," he answered. "Elis Francis."

"Elis," the Queen said. "You say you came here to make peace? Why would you do such a thing?"

"Because I don't see the reason in this conflict. Why must we, the people, be at odds with you, our queen?"

"You ask the rest of the townsfolk," the Queen spat. "I am not the one who started this fight."

"That does not mean you cannot finish it."

"Quiet!" The Queen rose from her throne, the animals spreading away from her. From behind the throne, Elis heard growling and he bowed his head again. "You dare judge my actions, which have saved many of my animals? Do you ever think about them, about the torture they've been through?"

"I think about them every day, My Lady. You must believe me. I am not here to judge, argue, or upset you, My Lady." Elis looked up at her. "I witnessed yesterday a tragic event. One of your snow tigers was captured by a chimney sweep. The tiger was freed but he left enough bloodshed to scare the whole town. Your tiger killed a man, My Lady. It is not your fault, nor the tiger's. It was his fault, the man in question."

"So it was you," the Queen said. "My tiger told me about you. You alerted him. He managed to contact me and I saved his life before it was taken."

"You gave him the strength of a queen," Elis said. He had not meant to sound accusatory, but the Queen looked furious.

"It was either that or my tiger would be the one dead on your streets," she hissed.

"With all due respect, they are *your* streets, My Lady."

From behind the throne the growl came again, and Elis watched – frozen in awe – as the snow tiger came forth and snarled at him. The Queen stroked the tiger's head.

"That incident is not the first in which humans have hurt my animals," the Queen said. "Stags have lost their lives, their antlers removed from their bodies. Butchers take rabbits, sheep, pigs. They take away my family."

"I apologise greatly, My Lady."

"Some are made to bleed to death; their limbs are hung out to dry. Some flesh is sold, eaten by inconsiderate brutes. Some are made into coats, or nice hats for people to wear. Some are even killed for fun."

The Queen stepped towards Elis, the snow tiger following her. She knelt and, with her finger under his chin, lifted Elis to his feet. Their eyes locked and Elis shuddered, feeling his face grow warm at her touch. He bit his lip to stop it quivering.

"Don't try to tell me my actions are fowl," the Queen said. "If you or anyone else insists on hurting the creatures I love, you deserve to be hurt in turn."

"My Lady, you have every right to look after your animals," Elis said. "But you are Queen. You must reunite with your people."

The Queen turned away from him.

"I understand you feel resentful towards them," he said. "But they are afraid. Though they have weapons, your animals have claws, teeth like glistening swords, and sharp minds to match. The people fear them. Or else they do not see their beauty. But it doesn't have to be this way. We humans and the animals – our lives are worth the same. Therefore, we must reunite. That is what I am begging of you."

"And you believe the townsfolk will listen?" the Queen said.

"Of course. Peace is all this town needs. Please."

Elis cupped his hands together. "Please, My Lady."

The Queen considered him, stroking the snow tiger's back. Then she said, "Leave us!" and like a burst the animals flew and raced out of the room. Elis was left with the Queen and, even without the presence of her guards, he was tense and aware of her power.

He lowered his head as the Queen stepped towards him once more. There seemed to be only the two of them in the whole world. As he looked at her, he noticed her face was calmer. She even managed a sad smile.

"I do not usually take on requests," she said. "Nevertheless, you did help in saving my tiger. He would not be here if you had not given him time to contact me. I will do as you suggest."

"Thank you, My Lady," Elis said.

"However, if you truly believe in making peace, then explain to me how I can approach the townsfolk. I cannot do this on my own."

"And I do not expect you to," Elis said. "I will gladly help you. I didn't come here without a plan."

"What do you have in mind?" queried the Queen. "You must prove to me your wisdom and kindness."

"Of course, My Lady, and that is exactly my plan! We must show the wisdom and kindness of your animals to the townsfolk, only then will the fighting cease. On my part, I will show you *my* peace. I have and will, forever more, obey and worship you. You may order anything of me and I will do it. I will never betray you or fall away from your side. You will always be my Queen."

"What do you have in mind?" the Queen repeated.

Elis caught sight of the purple rose in her hair

again. It kept her long fringe out of her face. When he saw it, he couldn't believe the sheer beauty of it. He couldn't believe the sheer beauty of her, the Queen.

"We bring them gifts," he said. "A gift no money can buy." He held up his hand. "Your flower. Where do you grow such exquisite flowers?"

"The roses?' the Queen said. "I am given them by my birds as tokens of gratitude. They pick them from a place where it is warm and where it never snows. Sometimes, I wish we had the power to grow these flowers in town."

"These flowers are the purity this town needs," Elis said in wonder.

"You wish for me to give these flowers to the people of the town?" the Queen said.

"Not just you, My Lady, but your animals too. They must have the courage to go into the town and give the gifts away."

The Queen's eyes lit up with fire. "You expect my animals to venture into a town where they are hated? They will be slaughtered. How dare you request such a thing!"

At once Elis fell to his knees and gripped the hem of the Queen's dress. He bowed right to the ground and closed his eyes.

"My Lady," he said. "I'll never wish to bring harm to your animals. Please hear me out. The gifts shall be given by your birds first. They can fly away if threatened. They can present themselves, and then leave. Then the smaller animals can emerge into town, followed by the larger, tougher animals. If the town greet them with open arms, we will have peace. You can be our Queen again." Elis took a deep breath. "And if I should ever betray you or break my promise in keeping your animals safe, you may bring the same pain that they will experience onto me. Endless suffering shall be my fate."

Elis gripped the Queen's dress tighter and his jaw quivered. He was patient in the silence as the Queen looked down upon him.

Somewhere in the distance, there came the faint sound of chirping. The chirping grew louder and suddenly a bird flew into the room. It was a robin, very much like one of the two that had greeted Elis at the front gates.

The small bird landed on the Queen's shoulder and pecked her neck as a greeting. The Queen turned to it and smiled. She hesitated, and then wove the rose free from her hair. The robin took the rose in its beak and Elis watched as it fluttered out through the window behind her, vanishing out into the cold.

Freedom to Lie
by Casey Armstrong

Nat still wasn't sure what had happened, what had changed as soon as Prohibition began. Sometimes she felt like Chicago itself had gotten into her bones and encouraged her. Despite the fear hanging over the city, she felt light. Maybe it was the dresses, layers of fabric gone, or the pounds of hair she had cut off (the hat she wore most days hid the way the relaxed curls fell around her ears).

It didn't take long for Nat to find Tom's, a quiet place downtown where conversation and music balanced each other out. Not long after she found it, it became the only place she went, with or without her friends. The dark wood floors covered in thick rugs and the gleaming bar decorated with comfortable furniture felt like home. Ellie, the owner and bartender, made sure of that. Whether it was a loud party full of dancing and live music or a regular night, she was always welcome.

Ellie was hard to miss. She was effervescent, with shiny hair that caught the light as she moved. It was impossible to not be charmed. She knew all the regulars by name, but her eyes followed Nat when she came in, especially as she danced.

"Natalie, darling," was her usual greeting as soon as Nat was close enough to the bar.

It was impossible not to return her smiles or to keep pushing the boundaries a little more each week. A brush of their fingers when she took her drink instead of letting Ellie push it across the bar, pulling her from behind the bar to dance on slow nights. There had been one memorable occasion, upon having one too many gin and tonics, where Nat leaned across the bar to press a kiss to Ellie's cheek, earning a chuckle from those watching and, more importantly, making Ellie flush pink. Nat could feel her own cheeks heat up upon doing that, and was glad she was dark enough to hide it.

There was no reason to consider the logistics of how exactly Ellie got her alcohol. It was illegal, but that hadn't stopped anyone. Besides, Nat was far too consumed with the prospect of Ellie and the glittery, clandestine world they both occupied to consider that. She didn't think anything of staying after close; she was more than willing to ignore the rumours that it brought about. Being able to talk to Ellie without anyone else around was worth it.

Ellie's brother Tom originally owned the place. It had hardly been open a few weeks when he was drafted, and he left it in Ellie's capable hands for the duration. He hadn't come home, but the bar lived on, going underground after the amendment had passed. Ellie had grinned when Nat said it was her favourite place; she knew Tom would be more than happy with how the place had turned out. The glimpses Nat got of Ellie, who Ellie was when she wasn't behind the bar, was enough to make her open up herself.

There was the struggle of finding a decent price for a whole chicken. The story of the time tomatoes had ended up on the bottom of the basket and so she had to make a sauce to hide the bruises. The pickiness of Mrs. Hudson's children (no one had ever disliked Mama's blackberry crumble until those little heathens).

It was a night in mid-September when Nat stayed later than usual. The customers had long since left and even the most stubborn of sticky spots on the floor had been scrubbed clean. It was far past time for her to leave. Ellie was glancing at her intermittently, waiting for her to make her excuses. Nat wasn't sure why she hadn't started the long trek home yet. She would hardly get any sleep as it was at this point.

There was something electric in the air, a feeling running through the room. Nat knew that if she stayed something was going to happen and she was more than a little curious as to what that might be. She had her guesses, of course; she knew what was brewing under the thin veneer of friendship.

"You alright, Nat?" Ellie asked.

"I have no place to be. Not like I'll be getting much sleep tonight, even if I leave right now."

Ellie glanced at the clock and swallowed hard. She hadn't realized the time.

"I didn't mean to keep you so late."

"I could have left if I wanted to," Nat reached out to touch her shoulder. "Just, at this point, there isn't much reason in going all the way home just to come back to this side of town in a few hours."

Ellie nodded. There was a long moment where Nat's thighs tensed as she readied to make for the door. Instead, as her brain slowed down a little, backed away from assumptions of the worst, and of the unspoken limits she knew should exist between them, she realized Ellie was putting together puzzle pieces in her head. Nat wondered what image they would form when she was done.

"It's a delivery night," Ellie said. "You're welcome to stay if you want, but I–"

Ellie didn't seem quite able to finish the thought.

"If it's easier for you, I can go."

"Nat, it's not just that. You're always welcome

here. I always want you here."

Ellie's mouth snapped shut. Nat felt like she had maybe said a bit more than she'd intended. She was rooted to her stool, trying to parse Ellie's meaning. She didn't know what Ellie was going to do, but Nat knew that, if it was her, she would have fled by now. But Ellie was holding her ground, and the air had grown thick around them. She watched as Ellie lifted the bar and gestured for her to come behind it. Ellie's eyes filled with disappointment when Nat remained rooted to her seat. She needed to move.

The sound of the bar dropping closed behind her made Nat jump. Ellie stepped towards her, not quite in her space, but close enough for it to send shivers down her spine. It took everything she had not to step forward.

"Ellie, what–?"

"I always want you here, but," Ellie found her voice again, "this part isn't... I don't have a lot of control over what happens. If things go wrong, I don't want you to get hurt."

"I know what you do."

"No, you don't. You see the fun parts, the reasons why I keep this place running, but the rest isn't as palatable. I may be good people, I like to think I am, but the people I have to work with, they aren't."

Nat wanted to reach for Ellie's hand, to reassure her that she'd do whatever it took to keep herself safe, first and foremost. It may have been a little bit of a lie though, so she kept her mouth shut for the moment, giving herself time to gather her thoughts.

Her curiosity was piqued. She didn't know if it was the danger, the potential of being caught (she could almost hear Mama telling her, that even up North, she had to be careful, that things were different for her) or if it was simply that she wanted to see a different side of Ellie. That she wanted to know every side of Ellie.

"I want to stay," Nat said.

"I just don't think business is for me. Maybe what Ken does, with the piano," Nat said.

The discussion had been ongoing since the first night Nat had stayed after hours. Ellie had asked what she would want to do if she didn't have the job she was currently working. It had ended up being a game of suggesting the worst possible jobs in the bar and figuring out reasons why they would be a good match.

"You know how to play piano?" Ellie asked, leading the way to the back door.

"I could learn. I'd rather be entertained sometimes than working all the time."

"I don't mind being bored. I like being behind the bar."

"I don't understand you, Ellie."

Ellie laughed, light and clear, and Nat smiled. Things had gone smoothly a couple nights previous, and Ellie had asked her to come back tonight. It was nice having someone to help move the crates up to the storage room. Ellie stopped just before the door. It took another minute for Nat's eyes to fully adjust to the dark room.

"Be safe tonight. If something happens, run, hide, do whatever you have to do so they can't find you. The cops or the runners."

"Of course." Nat bit back a laugh and ignored the thrill that shot through her.

It was dangerous. She knew that. She also trusted Ellie above everything else. She wouldn't be here if

Ellie thought there was any real risk of getting busted tonight. Of all the things to be afraid of, anything that involved Ellie wasn't it. With Ellie, Nat trusted she'd always be safe.

The hall was narrow. Even with both of them standing as they were, backs against opposite walls, they were close enough to touch. Nat could feel her breathing pick up.

"Natalie," Ellie said.

The world slowed down a little. Nat had spent a lot of time wondering if what she felt for Ellie was a product of rebellion, of wanting what she couldn't have. There had been a lot of nights she'd imagined Ellie's face, trying to suss out what was real. Here though, the glint of her eyes in the dark hall, the soft glow of her skin, she was sure. There wasn't any more doubt. It was definitely all Ellie.

Nat reached out, still half blind. She didn't have a plan but the need to do something forced her to take action. She jumped when she encountered warm fingers. Ellie was reaching out too. Nat realized she was about to jump off a cliff. Their fingers intertwined, warmth sinking into Nat's cool hands. Her breath hitched.

Ellie stepped forward. Nat could feel how warm she was, even through the soft cotton of her dress. She was so close now that Nat couldn't imagine pulling away. Ellie smelled like flowers, her perfume strong, but there was a hint of rum beneath it, where the scent of her job had sunk into her skin. Nat's free hand drifted to Ellie's hip, eyes fluttering closed at the give beneath them.

Ellie cupped her cheek as their breath intermingled. It was only a few more inches now. Nat rose up, closing the gap, barely brushing their lips together. Ellie's lips were soft and Nat wanted more. She pulled back, tongue darting out to lick at her lips, afraid she wouldn't taste Ellie again. Ellie's hand drifted to the back of her neck and she crowded further into Nat's space, pressing her against the wall. Nat's hand gripped her hip harder. Reflexively, Ellie leaned back in. The kiss was deeper this time; Ellie's tongue just barely pressing at the seam of her lips when a harsh knock startled them apart.

"Keep your head down, Nat."

Nat's hand lingered on Ellie's cheek and she leaned up for one more quick kiss.

"I will."

The metal door creaked as Ellie pushed it open. Whoever had knocked had already gone back down to the alley. Nat could make out a car, headlights off, in the shadows and reflections of the street lights. The sickly sweet smell of garbage, mostly refuse from the deli below Tom's.

A man was leaning against the car, dressed in a dark suit and needing the kind of lighting Chicago would never be able to provide. His hair was slicked back, the oil glinting and his lips curled in a sneer. There was a predatory glint in his eye that made Nat take a step back. Ellie ran a soothing hand down her back as she made her way down the stairs.

"Who's the broad?" he demanded.

"No need to worry about her," Ellie said.

"Wouldn't mind having a go at her then, if she's no one."

Ellie froze for a second. Then her arm snapped back and the resounding crack echoed down the alley. The man brought his hand up to his cheek and cowered under Ellie's glare. Nat understood what Ellie had meant now, that first night. This was dangerous and illegal, but the people involved were more dangerous than she could have imagined.

Nat backed up so she was standing a few stairs up. Being in the middle of this had become all too real. Ellie was holding her ground though, which was more of a surprise than it really should have been. Nat straightened her back and leaned against the railing, trying to find the bravery that was obviously planted deep within Ellie. Nat wasn't sure she had it herself – the decisiveness from last week had faded out at the threat – but she could at least fake it.

"This ain't that kind of place, Raymond, and you know it. I can find another supplier just as easily as I can keep using you."

"Like you would," he spat, but the words were undercut by the hand still at his cheek.

Nat took a deep breath. Ellie knew what she was doing. As long as Ellie was calm she was safe.

"Let's get this done so I can be in bed before dawn," Ellie said.

Ellie was all business now, any bit of civility gone. It was a new side of her. Somehow, the realisation that Raymond had a criminal element to him, if he wasn't flat out involved in organized crime, made Ellie slapping him that much more appealing. She had risked her business, and for all Nat knew, her life, in order to protect her. Still, she inched her way up the stairs to observe from the landing, not wanting to make a nuisance of herself.

"What's the proof on this stuff?" Ellie asked.

Her nose wrinkled in distaste as she sniffed a bottle. Nat knew her liquor, what went into each drink, but she was mystified by what Ellie was doing. She would have to learn later, but for now she let her attention wander. The view was nice. She could see a few blocks around and the city seemed to glow.

She almost missed the cars. The headlights were off and they were moving slowly enough that they were almost invisible. It didn't make any sense. It took a few beats longer than it maybe should have for Nat to put it together.

"Ellie!"

"What?" Ellie had jumped at the sound of her name.

"I think there's – There's a lot of cars headed this way, headlights off. I don't know."

"Shit." Raymond let out a few more expletives.

Nat's heart was rattling her ribs; she could practically hear it, and she had to take a deep breath to steady herself. She hadn't planned for this situation and she glanced at Ellie. Ellie was already looking at her, gears turning behind the tenderness of her gaze. While she waited for Ellie to find her voice, Nat pried her fingers off of the cold railing, ready to act.

"Nat, run," Ellie said. "You run and you don't come back here for at least a week."

"What about you?" Even in her panic, she knew she needed Ellie safe as much as she needed to keep herself safe.

"I'll be fine. Go!"

Nat obeyed, trying not to think. If she thought, she would freeze or do something equally stupid. The metal door slamming shut behind her seemed too loud for the situation, but there was nothing she could do about it. The fantasy of getting caught hadn't taken long at all to turn into a nightmare.

She kept a hand on the wall, trying not to trip.

They had left the minimum of lights on in the bar, though the hall was still dark and the contrast made it almost impossible to see. She grabbed her coat and hurried down the stairs. She scampered down to the deli and froze when she saw men, probably agents, milling around the door. Being seen wasn't an option. She waited until they were distracted, then slid into the kitchen and out the back exit. The alley was flooded with lights now and filled with more activity than it could hold.

Nat didn't let herself think until she was back home in her nightgown, safely wrapped in a blanket. She was shaking, hyperaware that she had gotten away by the skin of her teeth. She wasn't sure if she could live with that kind of risk. There was a lot to lose, and if she wanted this thing with Ellie to be her reality, she would have to start treating the work that went into running Tom's as more than a passing adventure.

If there would even be a Tom's after tonight.

She let out a shuddering sob, trying not to wake anyone. She couldn't explain it if she did. There was a chance Ellie had slipped away into the night. She might be fine, or at least as fine as she could be, knowing that her business, everything she had spent the better part of the last decade building up, was being destroyed. Alternately... Well, the alternative was her being shoved up against the rough brick of the alley before being hauled off to jail, and Nat wasn't sure she could handle even imagining that scenario.

Morning came far too quickly and after far too little sleep, but she had to go to work regardless. Her limbs were still heavy when she got on the streetcar.

Mrs Hudson was reading the newspaper when Nat arrived. She cast a panicked glance at the clock, afraid she was somehow late. She wasn't, so she hung her coat and set about making the coffee.

"Good morning, Miss Natalie."

"Good morning, Mrs Hudson. You're up early today."

"There was all sorts of racket last night. Liquor raids, according to the paper. They arrested a smuggler, Raymond Esposito, and a few others of his sort. It's a shame. I can't imagine what it's like in your neighbourhood, if this is happening in respectable places. I mean, it's part of the Constitution, and we have to respect that, if nothing else. Don't you agree?"

"Yes, ma'am. I find it best just to keep my head down. People will do what they're going to do, and there's not a lot I can do to convince them otherwise."

Mrs Hudson tutted under her breath. Nat was relieved she didn't seem particularly keen on continuing the conversation. She assumed the Raymond she had met last night was the same Raymond that had been arrested, which didn't bode well for Ellie's fate. Nat prepared Mrs Hudson's coffee and started on breakfast while she debated if she should ignore Ellie's edict to avoid Tom's.

"Natalie, are you going to the market today?"

"I was going to check after I finished breakfast. Did you need something?"

"If you would, pick up some beef for dinner tomorrow and some pastrami for Mr Hudson's lunches. Also stop by the creamery and increase the milk and butter order. There's the dinner party and then the family coming to stay."

"Of course."

Nat was glad to escape the house for a bit. It would be busy while Mrs Hudson's sisters were visiting.

"Nat," she heard, not two blocks away from the deli. "Natalie!"

She looked up, searching for the source of the noise. Ellie was waving from the third floor of the building Nat was standing in front of. It had to be her apartment.

"Ellie?"

"I'll let you in."

Nat wasn't sure how much time she had, but she would make something up, if she had to. She needed to see for herself that Ellie was safe. She hurried up the stairs once the door was unlocked. Ellie was waiting for her in the hall, door propped open with one foot. Nat ran down the hall, stopping just short of bowling Ellie down. Ellie ushered her inside, locking the door behind them. They took a moment, looking each other over, before Nat threw her arms around her.

"I'm glad you're safe," Nat said.

"I barely got away, ran as soon as I heard the door slam. All hell broke loose as soon as it did. I'm still not sure how they didn't see me."

"How did you manage?"

"Not a clue. There was a beat cop who questioned me when I was walking away, but I just, I don't know what came out of my mouth, but it worked."

"Ellie." Nat didn't know what she wanted to say, but she needed to say something.

"I told you to stay away, Nat."

"I was going to. I didn't know you'd be here. I

was just headed to the creamery to change the Hudsons' order for the month."

Ellie led her to the couch, and pulled her close so they were flush against each other.

"I'm so glad you're safe," Ellie said into her hair.

"What happened with Raymond?"

"It's not a huge loss. I was going to dump him after last night. There're plenty of other distributors out there. He's an ass."

"You're re-opening?"

Nat had been sure that Tom's was a thing of the past. Most places never bothered to re-open, and those that did usually moved. No one wanted to go to a place that had been raided. Consumption may not be illegal, but it didn't look good for most people either.

"It's what I do. I'll figure out who ratted us out, do repairs, restock. There will be a few changes, but I'm hoping a few of those might be positive."

"If you're sure, then let me know what I can do to help."

Ellie tapped Nat's chin, getting her to look up. She kissed her gently. Nat returned it, eager. She had been sure last night was a fluke. She was relieved it wasn't.

"I will. I have ideas. You came back, Nat. Most people wouldn't. I want you to keep coming back."

It was tempting to say yes to whatever Ellie wanted. Nat wasn't scared, not if she had Ellie with her. She didn't say anything, but she took Ellie's hand.

"Is it that simple?"

"For now. I have to wait for the heat to die down. You have work. We'll figure it out, Nat."

"Kiss me," Nat said. "Just to be sure."

It was different this time. Ellie was tugging her forward, kissing her with bruising force. Nat was practically in her lap, fingers tangled in Ellie's loose hair. She pulled back, and Ellie was kissing down her jaw and neck. Nat tugged her back up, bringing their lips together.

"I can't stay. I already don't know how I'll explain to Mrs Hudson why I took so long."

"Come back tonight, Nat."

"I will."

They exchanged a few more kisses before Nat forced herself to stand up, sparing one more kiss for Ellie's forehead.

Things were different when Nat visited Tom's these days. There were still some of the regulars, those who had come back after the raid at least, in their closely cut suits. They were perched on the stools, waiting to be pulled onto the dance floor by one of the girls. There were a handful of people she recognised, but who weren't there often enough for her to recall their names. Then there was also the rotating cast of men with guns on their hips and girls pulled to their sides scattered throughout the bar and dance floor and clogging up the back room. The churning feeling in her gut every time a new man came in had nothing to do with the fear she'd be kicked out if they kicked up a big enough fuss.

The fact that her nights started behind the bar now, with Ellie's kiss pressed to her cheek, was probably the only change that made her smile. Well, that and the fact she was well rested for once, having spent the night at Ellie's again. It was much closer, and not getting up at four everyday was doing wonders for her mood and her ability to tolerate Mrs

Hudson's sisters.

Tuesdays had always been slow and tonight was no different. The gangsters were out by ten and Nat finally felt like she could breathe and enjoy the next few hours with people she could consider friends. They trickled out and she watched the last of them close the door behind them.

She was only half surprised when a hand gripped her shoulder. She leaned up and wrapped her arms around Ellie's neck, pulling her into a slow kiss. They both laughed and watched the other for a moment, foreheads pressed together, before Ellie pulled back. She rubbed the back of her neck and pulled a few stray hairs back into place.

"It's a delivery night," Ellie said.

"It'll be fine. You've already gotten through one since the raid."

"I know. It's just part of the job. I can't look at it the same way now. It *feels* dangerous."

"It always was," Nat said. "I get that now. I'm nervous, too."

She knew it was probably the wrong thing to say. She twined their hands together, appreciating the contrast of their skin blending together in the shadows. There wasn't really a right thing to say and there wasn't anything she could do.

"I – would it be selfish if I asked you to stay until it was done? I want to walk you home tonight." Ellie was embarrassed to ask.

"Not at all. I'll stay as long as you want," Nat promised.

"Thank you. Wait up here for me?"

"It'll be fine," Nat said.

"I don't want to risk it. I haven't told you the deal I struck with them after the raid. Why they're here now, instead of down the road."

Ellie looked disturbed; her eyes were brimming with tears. Nat realized this was the first time she had seen Ellie scared. The new providers were the worst kind of bad news and Ellie couldn't say no for fear of another raid or worse.

"You don't have to tell me until you're ready to, Ellie. I'll be right up here though."

Waiting was always the worst part. Not knowing what was going to happen next. Nat remembered being fourteen and waiting for letters from her brother. Her mother scoured the newspapers for any word on the 9th Division, not hopeful they'd report it even if something did happen. Word of the battle reached them though, long before any news of Freddie did. When the telegram came, it was almost a relief. At least they knew – they weren't wondering anymore if they were going to see him again.

Sitting in the dark, perched on a bar stool, Nat couldn't help but wonder what Freddie would think of all this. If he'd have supported the amendment or if he'd be sitting here with her. The darkness was oppressive, pressing in tight around her. The streetlights and occasional passing headlights cast a dim yellow glow around her, but it wasn't enough to shake the feeling.

She settled for watching the cars and lights in office buildings click off. She could hear the voices in the alley. Men's voices, rough and grating, too loud for the task at hand. Ellie's gentler voice – sweet and melodic, but just as loud as the men's. Nat didn't dare move from her seat, afraid her silhouette would catch the wrong eye. Time had slowed to a painful crawl.

Eventually she heard a car door slam shut, metallic clang echoing up through the building. They had gotten through it. All that was left was making sure the distributor got back on the road (and stayed there) and hauling the product up to the back room. She heard the motor start and fade out. Nat stood, glad that she was going to be able to help now. She could hear Ellie's heavy footsteps making their way up the stairs, no doubt already carrying a case of gin.

The door swung open. Ellie wasn't carrying anything. Her hand was shaking so much she almost dropped the key. Nat pulled her in; making sure the door was shut and latched behind them. She guided Ellie to a stool and sat her down before going to get a glass of water. When she returned Ellie still had a white knuckle grip on the bar. She set the glass down and pried Ellie's fingers up until their hands were clasped. Ellie's breathing was still shaky, so Nat settled next to her, keeping their fingers intertwined and waiting until Ellie was ready. She took her time, sipping through half the water before colour started to creep back into her cheeks.

"I – Nothing happened. It was pretty normal, but the runners were new. I've never been so scared."

Nat stayed silent. She ran a hand through Ellie's hair, smoothing it.

"Nat, I don't think I can do this anymore. I need this to be legal."

"Then we'll find a way to make it legal."

THE FOX MOTHER
BY EMMY CLARKE

The Fox Mother lay next to her first creation. Though she had no eyes to see it, she felt the creation's fur next to her own. It was soft and fresh and new, and she loved it very much. It lay on her left side.

The Fox Mother lay next to her second creation. Though she had no eyes to see it, she felt the second, smaller creation's fur next to her own. It was soft and somewhat damp, and she loved it very much. It lay on her right side.

Because they lay on either side of the Fox Mother, her two creations were unable to touch one another.

The Fox Mother turned to her first creation and said, "Your sister has soft fur."

"I know," said the first creation.

"How can you know?" said the Fox Mother.

"Because I have soft fur," said the first creation.

The Fox Mother thought for a moment. Then she said, "Your sister is damp."

"I know," said the first creation.

"How can you know?" said the Fox Mother.

"Because I was damp when I was born, until you licked me clean."

The Fox Mother considered this. Then, smugly, she said, "She is bigger than you are."

"She is not," said the first creation.

"How can you know?" said the Fox Mother.

"Because I can see from here that she is half my size," said the first creation.

The Fox Mother growled and said, "How can you

see? I made you in my image. I have not given you eyes."

"And yet I see that she is small," said the first creation.

The Fox Mother stood up. Without another word, she walked away from her creations.

Refuge
by Ruth Woodward

I remember when we first arrived
I wondered how we would survive
Survive this dark and dismal place
Knowing the truth we'd have to face
Have to face the brutal truth
Admit that life was so uncouth
Face the reason that put us here
The future that we came to fear
The people that surrounded us
Didn't seem to make a fuss
I couldn't see how we'd fit in
It was like we were fit for the bin
We went upstairs and saw our room
The whole damn place seemed full of gloom
How would we get through these days?
The first week slipped by in such a haze
Of filling forms, and people asking why
We couldn't answer, although we'd try
The person who had put us here
Was living life as if in the clear
Clear of blame and worry free
While we were here, my daughter and me
Living under strict control
And worst of all, on the dole
My well paid job, I'd had to quit
To leave my home, and here I'd sit
Day after day I'd wonder why
Wonder why and often cry
How could he do those awful things
While I carried the guilt that he brings
The guilt of letting this be

Of letting him hurt my daughters and me
As the haze lifted, I could see we'd been gifted
With a chance to start again
Start afresh, soon but when?
The questions we faced were never ending
Some were truly mind bending
The rules we had to abide by
While he carried on without a sigh
Living with people we didn't know
My emotions I tried not to show
They asked me if I got upset
My answer always, "no not yet"
And if I did, I wouldn't tell
Never let you see me cry, or yell
I refused to break down and cry
While all the time they'd ask me why?
'Cos if I do then he'll win, and the true horror will sink in
I'll not let him destroy me, I'll fight through court, that you'll see
Once a month I had to go
To chart my feelings so they could show
That I was making progress here
This place where you should feel no fear
This place where hopes and dreams are made
Where people often start to fade
We often faced the doom and gloom
Curled up together in our room
That man he took our life away
With what he did that fateful day
But I wouldn't let him grind us down
My head held high when I went to town
The neighbours often looked our way
Knowing where we had to stay
Assuming we were all the same

Weak and useless, that's why we came
But the women here were very strong
'Cos men like him had done them wrong
Men that liked to think they ruled
Thinking we could not be fooled
Well I've had enough of your game
And now it's time you took the blame
I felt that we were doing time
Being punished for his crime
I remind myself we were in the right
So why did we every day have to fight
Fight to stop from going insane
We felt like we were inane
Days turned to months and we were still here
A place of our own seemed nowhere near
But then one day we were given hope
Given a lifeline, offered a rope
We moved into a flat of ours
No more wiling away the hours
A flat that we could call our own
Where we could finally be alone
No more rules for us today
We can do things our own way
Go to bed at our own time
Instead of "kids in bed by nine"
Our new life started here
But we still faced the fear
The fear that you would come
And then our new life would come undone
We started things as they should be
My daughters, my cat, the hamsters and me
Making a life where we could be
As happy as we really deserve to be
But still each day we had to face
The things you'd done to change the pace

I got a job, we settled down
In this unfamiliar town
A new school did my daughter start
And I felt within my heart
That maybe we could start anew
And live our life without you
The fear of seeing you in court
Often dominated my every thought
Of knowing your family would be there
Made me feel very aware
Of my fear that I'd crumble
Through the days I did stumble
But I knew, I would make it through
'Cos I wouldn't give in to you
I knew he wouldn't take the blame
Assumed I'd drop the charges cos I'm lame
Well how shocked were you that day
When you heard I was in court to stay
No screens, no video, did I need to plea
I wanted you to face me
Four hours long it took for me
To give my full testimony
Never once did I falter or stumble
Never did I lie, or crumble
Because I'd seen what you had done
And I knew you hadn't won
The day you tried to rape my daughter
And I knew that you oughter
Ought to pay for what you'd tried to do
The blame was never with her, it was you
You're the one who put us here
Yet you expected to be in the clear
Fifteen long months went by
Before the date came to try
To stand up in that witness box and say

Everything that happened that day
Private things I shouldn't have to share
But plead guilty you did not dare
So we all had to relive that awful night
What you did and how you did fight
Fight the officers sent to take you away
But I did not want you to stay
You were taken away from me
To a place you thought you'd never be
I thought you'd always be with me
You hurt my girls and that won't do
Never again would I trust you
So on that day as I stood in the witness stand
Scared as hell, but looking calm
As planned, I knew, I had to stay and face you in that court
Let you know I wasn't as scared as you thought
I could have hidden in a little room
Big enough to fit a broom
Or behind a screen, they said
But I wanted to face you in the flesh
To see you stood behind that glass
Acting as if you were bold as brass
But I know very well how you felt
I've known you long enough to tell –
You acted like you were hard, dead cocky
But I know inside you were rocky
I hate you for what you put us through
How much hate, you have no clue
Evidence given and home we went
Knowing your days in court were spent
Listening to what you had done
You hoped you wouldn't come undone
But come undone you did that day
When the jury came back to say

We find him guilty on that charge
I bet you wished you could have barged
Barged the security out of the way
Got in your car and ran away
So here we were two months down the line
Waiting to hear about your time
Will you go inside I say
Or be lucky and walk away
Whatever happens we both know
What you did and you will show
What sort of man you are
You're bad and evil, with no heart
What I'd give to make you see
What you've done to my kids and me
But for now I will wait
And let karma seal your fate

Meet the Storytellers

DIANE ENDERBY is a poet who doesn't know she is a poet. She lives with her rescue greyhound Little My and occasionally runs a marathon or two.

EVANGELINE CHATEAU-LONEY is a writer, editor, and blogger from Scotland. She has previously been published in Mslexia magazine and is very excited to be contributing to *Women of the Wild*. Contact her professionally via the MADA website or chat to her on Twitter @aufwader.

S. E. CYBORSKI has published a science fiction series, the ACCIDENTAL HEROES CHRONICLES, and is a published poet. She has been writing for as long as she can remember and still finds it a pure joy and pleasure. One she can't imagine life without.

HELEN NOBLE juggled motherhood and careers in law and psychology before her recovery from spinal surgery in 2011 forced her to sit still long enough to finish her first book TEARS OF A PHOENIX. Her collection of short stories titled SCORPIO MOONS followed, which includes her contribution to this anthology, RADIO GRANDMA.

L. S. REINHOLT lives in Denmark where she teaches languages and drama at a small independent school and spends most of her free time writing. She has tried her hand at many genres but science fiction is her greatest passion, having been raised on the works of Ray Bradbury and Jules Verne. She is currently working on her first novel with co-writer Minerva Cerridwen.

ALEX CLARKE is the founder of MADA indie publishers. She is also a produced playwright, screenwriter, and author. Her work is a mix of magical realism and the absurd. In 2017 she was awarded the Northumbria University/Channel 4 Writing for Television Award with her script BELOW and was mentored by Bonafide Films. Her short screenplay THE GIRL WHO DRESSED AS A BEAR was published in the 2017 *Hashtag Queer* anthology, available via Amazon.

GEMMA CARTMELL studies Music Composition at the University of Chichester. She is a wonderful and eccentric composer and writer of literature. Her inspiration comes from gothic, horror and weird fiction. Her favourite writers include: Edgar Allan Poe, Stephen King and Ian Banks.

CASEY ARMSTRONG is a writer working through Patreon. She focuses on historical fiction and speculative fiction, with current projects STOPPED, a WWI narrative, and TURQUOISE & QUARTZ, a fantasy epistolary. You can find her on Twitter @casey2y5 or screaming into a book.

EMMY CLARKE is a children's fantasy author who also dabbles in young adult fiction. She is part of the MADA team and is set to launch her own imprint in 2020. Her work includes LUCH & FRIENDS (available on Amazon and Lulu) and FOX FACE (available on Lulu). Her short story BRENNA appeared in the charity anthology *Unburied Fables* (also on Amazon). She hopes you've enjoyed reading *Women of the Wild* as much as she enjoyed editing and formatting it. You can find her wailing about books, D&D, cosplay and podcasts on Twitter @emmyaclarke or Instagram @starmaid.

RUTH WOODWARD is a poet living in the South West. She enjoys wiling the hours away by walking and also playing touch rugby.

Printed in Great Britain
by Amazon